His gaze shifted to the copper-haired young woman seated behind the desk.

Her lips curved in an inquiring smile. Mitch simply stared, his own lips curving in response.

The receptionist tilted her head and looked at him curiously. "May I help you?"

Mitch recovered his equilibrium enough to stride to the desk, hoping he hadn't lost credibility as a serious journalist. "I'm Mitchell Brewer. Mr. Showalter is expecting me."

Her blue-green eyes sparkled. "You have the eleven o'clock appointment, then. Please come with me. I'll take you back to Mr. Showalter's office."

Mitch followed along behind her, noting the way her hair changed color when she stepped into the shadows. With the sunlight pouring through the front window and glinting off her curls, the effect made him think of a new penny. Back here in the hallway, it appeared to be more of a strawberry blond.

He couldn't decide which shade appealed to him more, but he had no trouble approving of the way the curls followed the lines of her neck and spilled over her shoulder. Her trim figure moved along with a free, easy stride.

They passed through a small anteroom then stopped outside a closed door. His charming guide tapped on the door, then pushed it open.

"Mr. Brewer is here." She flashed Mitch a smile and stepped back to allow him to enter. Mitch felt his throat go dry. The scent of lilacs filled his nostrils when he brushed past her.

Nathan Showalter rose from his seat behind the massive walnut desk and extended his hand. "Brewer, it's good to meet you." He glanced over Mitch's shoulder. "By the way, Miss O'Roarke, that was a very nice piece you wrote. Keep up the good work." A delighted smile lit the receptionist's face before she closed the door and left them.

CAROL COX is a native of Arizona whose time is devoted to being a pastor's wife (of two churches!), homeschooling her young daughter, and staying in touch with her newly-married son and daughter-in-law. She loves any activity she can share with her family in addition to her own pursuits in reading, crafts, and local history. She also has had a number of novels and novellas published. Carol and her family make their home in northern Arizona. To learn more about Carol and her books, visit her Web site at: www.CarolCoxBooks.com. She'd love to have you stop by!

Books by Carol Cox

HEARTSONG PRESENTS

HP264—Journey Toward Home
HP344—The Measure of a Man
HP452—Season of Hope
HP479—Cross My Heart
HP580—Land of Promise
HP592—Refining Fire
HP632—Road to Forgiveness

Copper Sunrise

Carol Cox

Heartsong Presents

To Kevin and Samantha who also enjoyed an Arizona wedding.

Thanks go to Terri and Tony Watson, and Babs and Bill Porter, whose portrayal of the pioneers of Arizona gave me a glimpse of the excitement and wonder of Statehood Day.

A note from the Author:
I love to hear from my readers! You may correspond with me by writing:

Carol Cox
Author Relations
PO Box 721
Uhrichsville, OH 44683

ISBN 1-59310-938-5

COPPER SUNRISE

one

Phoenix, Arizona Territory—October 25, 1911

The portly man paced the length of the platform along the front of the Odd Fellow's Hall. A red flush suffused his ample cheeks, and his jowls quivered as he spoke to the assembled crowd. "And I say Taft has no right to impose his will upon us, president or not."

Loud applause greeted this pronouncement.

The speaker continued. "Ten months ago, the good people of this territory ratified the state constitution our delegates labored over so diligently. Two months ago, Congress passed a resolution for statehood. It is the God-given right of Arizonans to proceed to this next step in our destiny. We believe it, and the members of Congress believe it. If that rascal, Billy Taft—"

Loud *boos* burst forth from the audience, and he paused to let the interruption die down before he went on. "If that rascal, Billy Taft, hadn't vetoed that precious document, we might even now see the flag of the great state of Arizona fluttering in the breeze below the Stars and Stripes on the staff that stands before this very building."

Shouts of agreement mingled with huzzahs and loud cries of "Amen!"

In the back of the crowded room, Mitch Brewer scribbled in his notebook, anxious to capture every detail of this meeting for his readers back East. He scanned the assembly, writing brief descriptions of those present, everyone from laborers to well-dressed businessmen. Each strata of Arizona's residents seemed to be represented. A voice calling for quiet drew his attention back to the platform.

A slender, mustachioed man stood beside the previous speaker. Mitch recognized him as Nathan Showalter, a prominent Phoenix businessman. Showalter smiled at the audience with a practiced air. "Mr. Chilton makes some interesting points, and I must say I agree with him on a number of them." He paused, letting his words sink in.

"It's true that Arizonans voted to ratify the state constitution back in February. It's also true that Congress passed a resolution for statehood—a resolution subsequently vetoed by President Taft because of its provision for the recall of judges." He held up his hand to quell the boos that emanated at the mention of the president's name.

"I'm no happier than any of you at the idea of Arizona statehood being delayed one moment longer than necessary. After all, we've already waited nearly fifty years to see that day arrive. But I differ with Mr. Chilton as to what should happen next."

He stepped closer to the audience, positioning himself dead center at the edge of the stage, and waited. A hush fell over the crowd as the listeners waited for what would come next.

Mitch found himself as riveted as anyone there. The man was indeed a gifted speaker, he thought. He had to remind himself to look away from that piercing gaze long enough to continue his notes.

"Governor Sloan cautioned us about this very possibility after the ratification last February. He was sure the provision for the recall of judges would bring about the president's disapproval, and time has proven him right. But let us not forget that the president also signed the Flood-Smith resolution in August, which promises Arizona its rightful place in these United States. . .providing that provision is removed from the constitution by a vote of the people."

More boos followed. Chilton stepped forward as if to protest.

Showalter raised his hand, stopping Chilton in his tracks and quelling the crowd's rumbling in the same smooth motion. His tone sharpened. "Which is more important? To remain stiff-necked about keeping the constitution as it is. . .or for Arizona to become the forty-seventh star on the flag of this great land?"

A five-piece band near the front struck up a rousing rendition of "The Battle Hymn of the Republic," and the crowd went wild. Mitch could see Chilton's mouth opening and closing, but the man never stood a chance from that point on.

Mitch found his own heart racing in time with the martial air. Showalter had it right: Arizona had waited long enough for her day in the sun. The time had come to see her achieve statehood, and he would do anything within his power to bring that day to fulfillment.

He glanced back to the platform, where well-wishers had mounted the stage and were pumping the hands of both speakers. Assuring himself that the meeting was about to break up, he slipped outside the hall and hurried back toward the small house he rented, eager to write up his latest article.

The boardwalk echoed under Mitch's feet as he strode along, enjoying the balmy temperature finally setting in after months of searing heat. He breathed a sigh of gratitude that the meeting had been scheduled in the evening, giving him a chance to cover the story for the *Baltimore Sun* without causing a conflict with his job at the *Phoenix Clarion*.

A few weeks ago, it wouldn't have made any difference. Arthur Wilson, owner and publisher of the *Clarion*, understood and approved Mitch's desire to let the rest of the country see their quest for statehood from an insider's point of view. But ill health and advancing age forced Wilson to sell the paper.

The buyer, Lucas Dabney, didn't share Arthur Wilson's practice of spending time getting to know his employees. Up to now, Mitch's only contact with his new boss had been limited to perfunctory comments during their weekly staff meetings—hardly enough to make a good assessment of the man's probable reaction to knowing one of his reporters was also moonlighting for other publications. Dabney's no-nonsense demeanor and brusque way of speaking did little to boost Mitch's hopes the publisher would feel as warmly toward the thought as his predecessor had.

Still, Mitch knew he needed to let his employer know what he was doing. It was only right. In Dabney's place, he would want to be shown the same consideration. He promised himself he would bring it up the moment he spotted a good opportunity to do so. As much as he wanted to further the cause of Arizona's statehood, he didn't want to risk losing his job in the process.

Lonesome Valley, Arizona Territory—October 27, 1911

"What do you mean you're moving to Phoenix?" Dan O'Roarke planted his fists on his hips and stared at his daughter in dismay. "That's nearly a hundred miles away. What would make you want to put that kind of distance between you and your family?"

Catherine O'Roarke looked past her father and outside the wide front windows to the rolling hills that encircled the T Bar Ranch. For a brief moment she wished she could be out there, riding her mare down the length of Lonesome Valley and enjoying the peace outdoors rather than facing the tension that crackled here in the living room.

She stood with her back to the flagstone fireplace and considered her family's reaction to the announcement she had just made. Her mother's stricken expression came as no surprise. Neither did her grandmother's approving nod from the rocking chair in the corner. She'd known from the first that Grandma would agree.

Her father's reaction, though. . . She hadn't expected that kind of response from him. The disbelief in his tone made her bristle.

"Do you think I'm incompetent?"

The abrupt question cut off whatever her father might have been about to say. His jaw sagged, and he gaped at her. "No. Not at all."

"You think I'm incapable? Didn't you teach me to take care of myself?"

"Of course, but—"

A quiet chuckle interrupted him. Catherine's father swung around to face the diminutive figure in the rocking chair. "Do you see something funny in this, Mother?"

Fine lines webbed Elizabeth O'Roarke's cheeks when she smiled at her son. "Not in the sense you mean, dear. It's just that this whole scene brings back a flood of memories."

"Do these memories have any bearing on the fact that my only daughter has apparently taken leave of her senses?"

The older woman stared down at her lap as if collecting her thoughts. The rockers creaked against the pine floor, making the only sound in the room. Finally she raised her head and addressed them all, a nostalgic smile lighting her face.

"Hearing what Catherine has to say takes me back to the day I called my family together and told them I intended to travel to Arizona Territory to seek my fortune." Another chuckle gurgled from her lips. "My announcement created quite a sensation."

Catherine settled back on the raised flagstone hearth and wrapped her arms around her knees. She had grown up hearing the story of her grandmother coming to the territory as a young woman set on making her own way, but never before had she heard a whisper of a family altercation. She saw her father place his hands deliberately in his front pockets and recognized the effort it cost him to speak calmly.

"That's interesting, but it doesn't really pertain to what we're dealing with here."

"Oh, but it does." Catherine's grandmother leaned her head against the back of the rocker. She stared across the room with a distant look in her eyes as if she could see the scene from that long-ago moment playing out before her.

"If you and Amy are shocked at the thought of Catherine going out on her own today, imagine how my parents felt nearly forty-five years ago." A smile played across her lips. "I can understand their feelings better, now that I've lived long enough to see it from both points of view.

"I'd already arranged for a place to stay when I arrived here and intended to use the inheritance my grandmother left me to set myself up in business. I'd planned out the whole move in great detail. All that remained was to let my family know of my intentions and, hopefully, secure their blessing."

Catherine leaned forward eagerly. "And what kind of response did you get?"

Her grandmother smirked. "About the same as you're getting right now."

Catherine hugged herself and tried to contain her glee. Hadn't everyone always told her how much alike the two of them were? As long as she could remember, her mother had said that—usually with a note of resignation in her voice.

"We're both determined women," her grandmother continued.

"More like headstrong, if you ask me." Catherine's mother fixed her husband with the look Catherine had come to know as the "She gets it from your mother" expression.

"Call it what you like," Grandma went on, "but it all boils down to the fact that we're women of conviction. I knew I had to find my own way in life, and I believe Catherine feels the same way."

Catherine nodded in agreement, even though no one seemed to be paying much attention to her at the moment.

Her father sputtered. "But they're still having gunfights in the streets down in Phoenix."

"And just last week in Prescott, Hank Winters fired his pistol at Newt Thompson, right in the middle of the plaza," Grandma countered. "Human nature being what it is, you're going to find violence of some sort anywhere you go. A woman wanting to strike out on her own may not be the norm—"

"I should say not," her mother interjected.

"But it's far more acceptable now than in my day. Whereas I left Philadelphia to go to what my family called an untamed wilderness, Catherine wants to leave country life to go to the city." She grinned at her son and daughter-in-law. "And you two seem to feel that's just as frightening a proposition. A rather interesting turn of events, don't you think?"

From their grim expressions, Catherine could tell neither of her parents saw any humor in the comparison.

"But what will you do, Catherine?" Her mother's voice quavered. "At least your grandmother had some place to stay when she got here."

Catherine cleared her throat and stood, smoothing her blue worsted skirt with her palms. She glanced from her mother to her father. "As a matter of fact, I already have a job lined up." Buoyed by her grandmother's stalwart support, she strove to keep her sense of triumph from showing.

"I'll be employed at Southwestern Land and Investments, doing clerical work."

Her father's eyes bulged. "You're a ranch girl, born and bred. What do you know about that kind of job?"

"A ranch girl who spent her summers working in the office

at Sam Hill's hardware store. Remember how you always said the experience would help me later in life? I'm just trying to live up to your expectations."

A knock at the door prevented her father from responding.

Her mother pressed her hands to her cheeks. "Who could that be, at a time like this?" She hurried to swing the door open, then stepped back with a glad cry. "It's Alexander! Let's see what he has to say."

Catherine felt her mood lighten at the arrival of her lifelong friend. She suppressed a laugh upon seeing his bewildered look when her mother seized his arm and pulled him into the room.

"Good afternoon, Mrs. O'Roarke. I'm happy to see you, too." Alex's voice held its usual courteous note, but his gaze met Catherine's over her mother's head and demanded an explanation for the effusive welcome. Catherine only had time to send him a quick grin before her mother spoke.

"It seems Catherine has some notion about haring off down to Phoenix." She tugged him farther into the room. "You, of all people, know how stubborn she can be, but you've always been able to make her see reason. Talk some sense into her, will you, Alexander?"

The grin slid from Catherine's lips. She and Alex had grown up together, playmates and adversaries by turns. He had been both her best friend and her nemesis, and at times she felt closer to him than to her own brother. He wouldn't be any happier than her family about her perceived desertion. She braced herself, waiting for him to second their opinion.

Alexander's deep blue eyes fixed Catherine with a steady gaze. After a silence that seemed to last an eternity, he moistened his lips. "I can't say I'm surprised. I guess I've always known Catherine would want more out of life than she could ever find here. She has bigger aspirations than our rural life could ever meet."

He crossed the room to stand beside her. "I don't know what happened to make it all come together just at this time." He reached out to clasp her fingers and gave her a warm smile. "But I'm behind you a hundred percent."

"But—but. . ." Her mother's lips twisted. "I always thought the two of you—" She clapped her hand to her mouth.

Her obvious embarrassment sparked a wave of pity. Catherine spoke quickly to fill the awkward silence. "No, Mother. We've always been good friends, but that's all we'll ever be. If I ever decide to marry, I'll look for a husband who stirs my heart and knows how to treat a woman." She slanted a playful glance at Alexander. "Not someone who may take a sudden notion to dump ants down the neck of my dress."

"Catherine Elizabeth!" Her mother wore a look of horror.

Alex laughed and held up his hands. "That was a long time ago."

Catherine chuckled along with him. "Yes, but I've never forgotten it, and apparently you haven't either." She smiled, her earlier tension melting away. "Honestly, Alex, would you want to begin a marriage with a wife who harbors so many memories or start fresh with someone who won't discover your worst qualities until after the wedding?"

"Catherine!" Her mother plopped down into a chair and fanned herself with her hand.

Alex wrapped his arm around Catherine's shoulders in brotherly fashion. "No offense taken, Mrs. O'Roarke. Catherine has a point. But then, she usually does." He fixed Catherine with a look of pride that made a lump form in her throat.

It would be hard to leave a wonderful family and a friend who knew her nearly as well as she knew herself. But her future didn't lie here. Her dreams led her to the bustle of life in the territory's growing capital city, not the slow pace of the ranch she'd always known as home.

Their levity seemed lost on Catherine's mother. She turned to her husband with a pleading expression. "What shall we do, Dan?"

Catherine's father scraped his hand across his cheek. "Beats me." He stood a moment in thought, then turned to the white-haired woman in the rocker. "Mother, you said you could see the situation from both sides now."

Grandma rocked placidly and nodded. "As a young woman, I only understood that I felt compelled to go. A grand adventure lay before me, something that stirred my blood and made me feel alive." Her voice softened. "I know how Catherine feels, but until I had children of my own, I couldn't begin to realize the anguish my parents went through. They must have—"

"Aha!" Father's cry of triumph cut through the room. "Then as the one person here who's qualified to understand both points of view, please tell us what you think we should do."

His mother favored him with a gentle smile. "You didn't let me finish. They must have spent many a sleepless night worrying about what might happen to me. While I'm sorry for the pain I surely caused them. . .I know I made the right decision. God watched over me then. You can trust Him to watch over Catherine, as well."

Only the creaking of the rockers could be heard in the silence that followed. Catherine held her breath.

Her father looked at his mother uncertainly. "Then what you're saying is. . ."

Grandma nodded. "Let her go."

two

The crisp fall breeze grazed Catherine's cheeks. She shivered slightly and pulled her shawl closer around her shoulders. Wrapping one arm around the trunk of a cottonwood tree, she rested her head against its rough bark.

The branches dipped in the wind, shaking loose some of the last few clinging leaves and sending them swirling. Days might still be sunny, but autumn was definitely making its arrival felt.

What would autumn and winter be like in Phoenix? Her family had visited Tucson twice while she was growing up, both times during the fall. Remembering those childhood trips brought back thoughts of happy days spent riding across the desert and picnicking in Sabino Canyon, but few memories of passing through the capital city.

Another gust of wind set more leaves free. Catherine watched them skitter across the tops of the bunch grass, wanting to fix the familiar view in her mind forever. As eager as she felt to begin her new life, this land would always be a part of her.

Their neighbor, Jacob Garrett, had grown up in the desert. When she'd asked him what to expect, he laughed. "You can count on two things from the weather there: hot and hotter."

What would it be like to go through an entire year without the changes in seasons she expected as a matter of course here in the northland?

I don't have to leave. I could stay right here and go on being the same person I've always been. The thought turned her stomach sour. She could never do the things she wanted—no, needed—to do if she stayed here.

Catherine squared her shoulders. This was the right move for her. It had to be.

Could it be that I'm just bullheaded, like Mama says? Maybe I'm making a huge mistake.

"No!" The word sprang aloud from her lips.

"Talking to yourself?"

Catherine spun around to see her brother, Ben, standing only a few feet behind her. "Where did you come from? I thought you'd gone to look at that bull in Holbrook."

Ben tipped his hat back on his head in a familiar gesture. "I just got back. It sounds like I missed quite a wingding while I was away. You really managed to set the family on its ear."

Catherine tilted her head to look up into his suntanned face. "You've talked to Dad and Mama already?"

"No, I ran into Alex in town when I got off the train. He filled me in on the whole thing." He picked up a dry stick from the ground and started breaking it into pieces. "So why are you really taking off, Sis? I never realized you hated living here."

"I don't hate it. . .not exactly. I just can't stand to be cooped up here anymore."

"Cooped up?" Ben cast a puzzled glance at the wide-open vista around them.

Catherine had to laugh at his expression. "It does sound foolish, doesn't it? But that's how I feel. It's like I'm a bird in a cage, and I have to break free."

"I still don't get it." Ben tossed the remnant of the stick away. "You mean you're bored?"

"That isn't it, either. Who could be bored looking at this every day?" Catherine swept her arms wide to indicate the vast panorama. "There's always something new to see—leaves changing colors in the fall, snow dusting the ground in the winter, the new calves every spring. . ." Her voice trailed off, and she swallowed hard. Leaving it all behind wouldn't be as easy as she'd thought.

"You're tired of the people around here, then?"

Catherine ran through a mental list of the people in her life: her parents and grandparents; Ben; Alex; their friends, Jacob and Hallie Garrett; people from their church.

"No." Her voice caught in her throat. "No, they're the salt of the earth—steady, stable, unchanging. . . . That's it, Ben. Nothing ever changes."

"But you just said—"

She shook her head impatiently, eager to explain the thought that had just taken shape in her mind. "I know what I said, and it's true; there's always something happening. But it's always the same things over and over. It's so predictable. I know exactly what to expect.

"Out there. . ." She braced her hands against the cottonwood trunk and gazed toward the Bradshaw Mountains to the south. "Out there, things are happening. Big things, and I want to be a part of them. I *have* to, Ben. I have more to offer to the world—to myself—than just staying here and stagnating."

Ben chuckled. "So what are you planning to do that's going to set the world on its ear?"

"Maybe nothing right away, but at least I'll be down there where things are going on. You never know what opportunities might come from this job. I see it as just a beginning."

"Tell me about this grand new job of yours. How did you find out about it, anyway?"

Excitement bubbled up inside her at the chance to explain to someone who was truly interested. "I was talking to the Stapleys awhile back. You know, that new family who moved here a couple of years ago. It turns out they lived in Phoenix before they moved up here, and Mr. Stapley knows tons of influential people down there."

Ben nodded. "Go on."

"When I happened to mention that I'd be interested in working down there someday—"

"You just 'happened' to mention that, eh?"

"Okay, I may have steered the conversation that way a bit, but I was only looking for information. I never dreamed it would lead to anything like this."

"I still don't see how that was enough to land you a job."

Catherine smiled, still amazed at the way it had all come together. "Mr. Stapley gave me the name of a man he knows. I sent him a letter, telling him about my qualifications, and he wrote back right away saying I sounded like just the kind of person he was looking for to work in his office." She straightened proudly. "I'm going to be working for Southwestern Land and Investments." The name rolled off her tongue. "Doesn't that have an impressive ring?"

The corners of Ben's mouth twitched, as if he were trying to hold back a grin. "Exactly what does this impressive company do?"

"It's a land development firm. And the owner, Nathan Showalter, is a very forward-thinking man, or so Mr. Stapley says."

Ben's face darkened. "He'd better not be forward thinking when it comes to my sister."

Catherine scowled and gave him a little shove. "You sound just like Dad. It isn't like you're sending some helpless little lamb into a lion's den, you know. I can take care of myself. I've done that plenty of times right here around Prescott. It's a respectable job with a perfectly respectable company."

Ben hooked his fingers in his belt loops. "So what does this job involve?"

For the first time, Catherine faltered. "I'm a little shaky on the details. I know I'm to have my own desk and work on some big projects. But that really isn't the point. The important thing is that great things are ready to break open for this territory. We're about to become a state, Ben, just think of it! And I'll have a front row seat for everything that's going on. No more just watching things happen; I'll be part of *making* things happen."

"Right there from your little desk?" Ben tugged on her hair, just the way he'd done when she was a little girl.

Catherine wrinkled her nose. "All right, maybe my job won't have a direct bearing on getting us to statehood, but I'll be there in the capital where it's all happening. Why, there's even talk of women getting the vote in Arizona. Imagine!"

"That idea was voted down during the constitutional convention, little sister. Or have you forgotten?"

Catherine lifted her chin. "Not at all, dear brother, but in case *you've* forgotten, the constitution provides for bringing initiatives before the people, and plans are in motion to do exactly that—bring the matter of women's suffrage up for a public vote. Maybe I can be a part of that. Wouldn't Grandma be proud?" She clapped her hands. "It's wonderful, the way God is bringing all this about."

Ben regarded her thoughtfully. "You're sure this is God's doing?"

She pushed her earlier misgivings aside. "Of course! Just look at the way all these things have come together." She ticked off each point on her fingers as she spoke. "The Stapley family just happens to move up here. I just happen to meet them. Then we just happen to be talking about working in Phoenix, and Mr. Stapley's acquaintance just happens to need someone to work in his office at that exact time."

She beamed a triumphant smile. "Those are far too many things to be called coincidence, Ben. Can't you see God's hand at work in this?"

Ben paused a moment before answering. "I'm not saying

it isn't, but I think the Lord gets the blame a lot of times for things we orchestrate ourselves."

"Not this time. I feel it. This is meant to be; don't you understand?"

Ben shook his head slowly. "No, Sis, I can't say I do." He slung his arm around her shoulders and squeezed her tight. "But I'll back you anyway."

❧

"You wanted to see me?" At a gesture from his boss, Mitch stepped inside the cluttered office and shut the door against the clatter of the linotype.

Lucas Dabney continued scribbling on the pad in front of him and waved Mitch to a chair on the visitor's side of his desk.

Mitch settled into the ladder-back chair, mildly irritated at being summoned while ideas for his current story were coming in full flood. He shifted on the hard seat and jiggled his right foot.

Dabney scratched down a few more lines, then set his pen and pad to one side. Resting his arms on his desk, he laced his fingers together and stared at Mitch without speaking.

Mitch quit fidgeting and started worrying. Dabney had something on his mind—but what?

"Seems like the whole country is talking about Arizona these days," Dabney said at last.

It took Mitch a moment to find his voice. "You're right. It's the talk of the nation." He found it hard to believe his boss had called him in for nothing more than light conversation. On the other hand, maybe he'd decided to spend some time getting to know his employees better.

Mitch relaxed a fraction, but his conscience prodded him. Now would be a good time to tell Dabney about his outside activities. He owed him that as a good employee—even more as a man of integrity. He'd put it off too long already.

Dabney leaned back in his oak chair and propped his feet on the corner of his desk. "In fact," he went on, "you can hardly pick up any of the eastern papers without seeing something about Arizona's and New Mexico's quest for statehood."

The moment had come. Mitch cleared his throat. "Yes, and speaking of that—"

"I've started saving some of the better articles I come across." Dabney lowered his feet to the floor and slid open the top left desk drawer. "These ought to make an interesting collection someday, don't you think?"

Mitch's mouth went dry at the sight of a thick stack of clippings. What were the chances this conversation wasn't heading in the direction he feared it was? "They'll make quite a scrapbook. And while we're on the topic, I need to—"

Dabney's face took on a bland expression Mitch immediately found suspect. He stirred through the clippings with his forefinger. "Good stories, these. There's some real talent out there. This writer, for instance—his name seems to keep popping up." He withdrew one neatly trimmed article from the stack and sailed it across the desk.

Uh-oh. Mitch trapped the clipping beneath his palm. He lifted his hand and stared at the paper, seeing the very words he prayed he wouldn't: RACE FOR STATEHOOD TIGHTENING UP ran the headline. Below it was the byline—Mitchell Brewer.

Mitch stared at the incriminating proof for a long moment, then raised his head and looked straight at Dabney. "I owe you an apology. Mr. Wilson knew I was doing these pieces for other papers, and he was fine with that. But I should have let you know right up front, and I didn't. I assure you all of them were written on my own time after my regular hours here." He fought the impulse to assure his boss he was a man of honor.

His actions hadn't exactly demonstrated that. He braced his hands on his knees and waited for Dabney's response.

His employer held his gaze with a long stare, then a glint of humor quickened in his eyes. "All right, I've had my fun. I guess it's time I let you off the hook. Wilson told me you were a go-getter. Just so you know, I happen to agree with him. . . and I'm very happy for you."

Mitch sagged in the ladder-back chair. "Thank you, sir. I appreciate that."

"You're doing the *Clarion* proud. Keep up the good work."

Mitch stared. This went beyond anything he'd hoped for. "You mean it?"

Dabney's typically brusque demeanor returned. "Of course I meant it! It doesn't do the *Clarion* a bit of harm for people to know we have a writer of this caliber. I'm just glad you didn't decide to go to work for the *Arizona Republican* instead."

Dabney stood and walked around to the front of the desk. "More than that, it's good for Arizona. And remember, Brewer, we're on the brink of something big here, something far bigger than ourselves. I wouldn't feel right about hoarding your talent for myself when statehood is so close to becoming a reality."

Relief made Mitch light-headed. "I feel the same way. About this being something big, I mean. Covering this story is a once-in-a-lifetime opportunity."

Dabney nodded, and his expression grew even more sober. "What are your plans over the long run? With your talent, I can't expect you to want to continue working for the *Clarion* for the rest of your career."

The last of Mitch's tension drained away. He hitched his chair forward, eager to share his dreams with someone who would understand. "None of this was planned. I sent a brief article on the constitutional ratification and Taft's veto to a Philadelphia paper, and they asked for more. Then I sold a piece to the *Boston Herald* and one to the *New York Post*, and the whole thing kind of snowballed after that."

Mitch stood and paced the width of the office. "I want to keep up the momentum, but I'm not quite sure how to do it. I'd welcome any suggestions you might have."

Dabney leaned against the corner of his desk. He narrowed his eyes and stared at the opposite wall, his fingers drumming lightly on the desktop. "What about profiles? Something to let the rest of the country get acquainted with the leaders in politics and business. Show them the movers and shakers around here."

Dabney crossed the office and gripped Mitch by his shoulder. "That's it, my boy. You have the opportunity to dispel the notion once and for all that Arizona is full of outlaws and ruffians. Our delegates to Washington have been trying to do that for years, but with your talent, you may be just the one to accomplish it."

Mitch felt his heart beat faster with mounting excitement. "Maybe God put me in this place at this time for just this purpose." He stared into space, trying to sort through the whirl of ideas that suddenly presented themselves.

Dabney's voice called him back to the moment. "Well, what are you doing, just standing there? Get out of my office and get started!"

three

Catherine detached herself from the crowd moving along Jefferson Street and stopped in front of the building bearing the name SOUTHWESTERN LAND AND INVESTMENTS. With a growing sense of delight, she studied the name in gilt lettering on the front windows of the neat, red brick building and caught her breath at the wonder of it all.

She, Catherine Elizabeth O'Roarke, stood ready to take her place in the world.

Catching sight of herself in the plate glass, she took a moment to examine her reflection. Her white blouse and matching navy skirt and jacket made her look businesslike yet feminine. Catherine nodded approval. She would fit right in with the city scene.

And her mother thought she would be content to stay up north and marry Alexander Bradley! Catherine shook her head at the absurdity of the idea. Once he got past slipping those ants and the occasional frog down the back of her dress, Alex had been a good friend to her. He was one of the kindest, most dependable people she knew, and he would make a fine husband. . .for someone else.

But ranch life suited Alex. He would be forever happy tending his cattle and raising a passel of sons to follow in his footsteps. She, on the other hand, would die, simply *die*, if she had only that to look forward to for the rest of her days.

A motor car tooted its horn, sending a clutch of pedestrians scurrying out of its way. Everywhere she looked, people hurried to and fro as if each one was bent on an important task. The very air crackled with a sense of urgency. And it suited her to a T. Bolstered by that knowledge, she walked up the steps to meet her destiny.

Inside the small foyer, Catherine took a moment to let her eyes become accustomed to the dimmer light. . .and to quell the surge of anxiety that took her unawares. Trying to effect an appearance of poise, she walked across the hardwood floor to the reception desk opposite. The rather plain young woman seated there looked up. "May I help you?"

"Good morning. I'm Catherine O'Roarke. Mr. Showalter is expecting me. I'm to begin working here today." She surreptitiously slipped her handkerchief from her sleeve and kneaded it in her hand.

The receptionist flashed a friendly smile. "Miss Trautman will be your supervisor. I'll go let her know you're here."

She disappeared through an archway in the back wall and came back a moment later, accompanied by an older woman wearing spectacles on a chain around her neck. "Miss Trautman, this is Miss O'Roarke."

Catherine studied the supervisor. She held her head and shoulders drawn back in a way that reminded Catherine of a pouter pigeon. Catherine bit her lower lip to stifle the desire to laugh. Her gaze dropped to the other woman's impeccably tailored outfit, and her heart sank. Her own clothes looked positively frumpy in comparison.

Miss Trautman swept her from head to toe with a look that made her feel like an unwanted intruder. *Mr. Showalter gave me this job*, she reminded herself. *I didn't come here as a beggar.* She drew courage from the thought. Lifting her chin, she stared straight back and waited for the other woman to speak first.

"Ah, yes. The little girl from the ranch. I'm sure this will be a great change for you." Her eloquent look said she doubted Catherine would be up to the challenge. "Follow me, please."

Catherine bit back a hot retort. She was part of the business world now, and such remarks had no place here. She followed Miss Trautman through the archway and down a hall to a spacious room where two young women worked diligently at their typewriters.

"This is your new coworker, Catherine O'Roarke," Miss Trautman announced without preamble. Turning to Catherine, she added, "These are Enid and Irene."

The women glanced up long enough to send quick smiles Catherine's way, then resumed clattering away at their machines.

Miss Trautman led the way to a desk in the far corner of the room. "This is where you'll be working. Wait here a moment." She returned to the door and called, "Mattie, please come here."

When the receptionist arrived, Miss Trautman told her, "Miss O'Roarke will be taking on the responsibility for writing advertising copy. I'll watch the reception desk while you explain the nature of her work to her."

A pleased expression spread over Mattie's face. She turned to Catherine. "I can't tell you how glad I am to have someone take over this job. It fell into my lap when Ruthie left, but I just don't have a talent for it."

Miss Trautman sniffed in evident agreement with Mattie's statement then left. Mattie watched until the door closed behind her then turned to Catherine again. "Ruthie couldn't seem to stay on Miss Trautman's good side. To tell the truth, though, we all have trouble with that." She ended on a muffled giggle.

Enid glanced up from her typewriter. "And if you don't want to wind up like her, you'd better watch what you say around here."

"She's right, you know." Mattie lowered her voice to the faintest whisper. "That woman has ears like a fox. You have to be careful not to say anything to set her off."

"I'll try to remember that." Catherine tried to recapture her earlier optimism enough to respond to the twinkle in Mattie's sharp, dark eyes. "I'd better get started, then. What exactly am I supposed to be doing?"

"Here, let me show you." Mattie walked to a bookcase set against the wall near Catherine's desk and stood on tiptoe to pull a bound volume from the top shelf. Hefting the heavy book in both hands, she set it on the desk with a thump and opened the cover to reveal pages filled with clippings of ads arranged in scrapbook style. "You'll be writing copy for ads like these. The company places them in the papers back East to draw investors."

"I see," Catherine said, hoping she sounded more confident than she felt.

"If you want my advice, I'd suggest you spend today just going through the book and reading the copy here to see the kind of thing we've already done and familiarize yourself with the different properties Southwestern represents."

Catherine found herself nodding. "That's a good idea. I wouldn't have the slightest notion where to start otherwise. How many ads do we have running at any one time?"

"More than you think you can handle, but never enough to satisfy Mr. Showalter. We're entering new markets all the time." Mattie made a face, and Catherine laughed. Mattie might not be a fashion plate, but her down-to-earth way of putting things made Catherine feel a little more at home.

Mattie straightened some pencils on the desk then looked up. "Miss Trautman said something about you living on a ranch. Is it near here?"

"No, the T Bar is up near Prescott."

Mattie's eyes grew round. "Oh, then you're a long way from home. When did you get into town?"

"Just last night." A sudden wave of homesickness caught her by surprise. Had it only been a day since she bid her family good-bye at the depot?

"You've hardly had time to get settled, then. Where are you staying?"

"The Bellmont Hotel."

"The Bellmont?" Mattie echoed. "You can't afford to stay there very long. Those prices will eat you alive. Unless, of course, you're used to spending that kind of money. But if you are, then what are you doing working here?" Her saucy grin took any sting from her words.

Catherine remembered the sinking feeling she had the night before when the desk clerk told her the room rate. The Stapleys had recommended the Bellmont as a respectable place, well suited for a young woman. But apparently respectability came at a price, one Catherine wouldn't be able to afford for long.

She looked straight into Mattie's friendly eyes. "The truth is, I can only stay there another night or two. I'm living on my savings until my first payday, and that won't last long at the rates they charge. I need to find someplace cheap but decent. Do you have any suggestions?"

Mattie's face lit up. "There's a room available at my boarding-house. It isn't anything fancy, but the price is right and the food is good. Would you like to stay there?"

A wave of relief made Catherine's knees go weak. She plopped down into her chair and smiled up at Mattie. "I'd like that very much. Thank you."

Mattie winked at her. "I'd better get back to the front before Miss Trautman has a conniption. Come see me if there's anything you don't understand. I'll go with you to your hotel after work and help you move your things to Mrs. Abernathy's house."

"Don't I need to meet her first and give her a chance to see if she approves of me?"

"She'll approve, all right." Mattie's confidence left no room for doubt. "She'll be glad to have you there, and you'll love her. Mrs. Abernathy is a fine Christian woman. You'll feel right at home."

Catherine stole a glance at the two other women after Mattie left, but they kept their heads bowed, hammering away at their machines. She pulled the book of clippings in front of her and began to study the advertisements.

Renewed excitement bubbled up inside her. She held a meaningful job in the territorial capital, right in the thick of things. And from the descriptions of the company in the ads, Southwestern Land and Investments was poised to play an important role in Arizona business matters in the days to come.

Wouldn't the folks back home be impressed when she told them about her wonderful job? Thanks to Mattie, she'd also be able to let them know she would be taking a room with a fine Christian landlady. Perhaps she would pen a letter home that very night.

A stimulating job, a respectable place to stay, and a new friend. Not bad for her first twenty-four hours on her own. With a contented sigh, she bent over the clippings and resumed reading.

Before long, she found herself engrossed in flowery descriptions of business properties and irrigated farmlands. The more she read, the more her excitement grew. This wouldn't just be a job; this would play a vital role in Arizona's future. She would be a part of history in the making.

❧

"Friday at one, then. That will be fine. Thank you very much."

Mitch put the telephone earpiece back on its hook and

reached in his pocket for his pencil. Another interview to jot down on his rapidly filling calendar. He should feel jubilant at the reception his idea was getting among the subjects for the profiles he planned.

He went back to his desk to scribble a note about the time and place, then rested his elbows on the desktop and pinched the bridge of his nose between his thumb and forefinger. All he felt right now was tired. Just plain dog tired.

He had to hand it to Lucas Dabney; that idea about writing the profiles had been a stroke of genius. And Dabney pulled out all the stops on cooperating with this venture, giving pointers and assigning Mitch to stories with a political focus. His own father couldn't have given him more encouragement and support.

Now if he could just figure out how to squeeze another twelve hours into each day.

After spending a full working day chasing the stories his boss so thoughtfully handed him then working late into the night on his articles for the eastern papers, he'd begun to wonder just how long a man could get along on three or four hours of sleep each night.

It didn't matter. An opportunity of this magnitude might never come again. He didn't intend to be guilty of spurning a God-given chance to further his career.

One of the office boys threaded his way through the desks in the large room. "Got a letter for you, Mr. Brewer." Without slackening his pace, he gave a flick of his wrist and spun an envelope onto Mitch's desk.

Mitch stretched his arms wide and rolled his neck from side to side before picking up the letter. Wedging his finger underneath the edge of the flap, he ripped it open and pulled out the single sheet of paper.

He glanced at the signature at the bottom of the page and

grinned. Alex Bradley—he hadn't heard from his friend up north in quite a while. Mitch propped his feet on his desk, deciding to take a welcome break and find out what Alex was up to.

Dear Mitch,

Long time, no hear. Hope things are going well with you. I'll get right to the point of this note. Do you remember me talking about that little spitfire I grew up with? Well, the little spitfire has turned into a woman with a mind of her own, all grown up and quite capable of taking care of herself—or so she keeps saying to anyone who'll listen.

My point in telling you all this is that she's managed to land herself a job down your way. If you think this is leading up to my asking you for a favor, you're right. Would you mind checking up on her for me? I'm sure you can come up with a plan to do it in such a way she doesn't suspect I sent you. And that's important—make no mistake about it. Who knows what she'd do if she thought I put you up to this! You don't need to go to any great lengths. Just make sure she hasn't gotten herself in some kind of mess. If she has, I know her well enough to know she'd be too proud to ask for help after her declaration of self-sufficiency.

In all probability, she's getting along just fine, and I'm acting like an overprotective big brother, but the truth is, she really is like a little sister to me, and I hate to think of her being down there all alone without anyone to watch over her.

I don't know where she's living, but her job is with the Southwestern Land and Investments Company. When you've found out what her situation is, write and let me know how she's doing, will you?

By the way, I came across a copy of a collection of Billy Sunday's sermons. Have you had a chance to read them?

If so, I'd like to compare notes and get your views on his
method of spreading the gospel. Wouldn't it be something
if we could all have an impact like that!

Thanks in advance for checking up on my "little sis." Her
name, by the way, is Catherine O'Roarke. Hope to hear soon
that all is well and my concerns are groundless.

Regards,
Alex

Mitch stared at the letter a moment, then folded it neatly
along its creases and tapped the corner on his desk. He'd known
Alex for several years, long enough to be sure he wouldn't ask
something like this unless he really felt it necessary.

But when was he supposed to find time to run this little
errand? A knot of tension formed in his chest. He had more than
enough to handle just trying to do interviews and write articles in
between job assignments.

He went over the letter again. From the sound of it, this
girl had plenty of spunk to be able to handle herself nicely.
Moreover, she wouldn't be likely to welcome a stranger sticking
his nose into her business.

Mitch sat upright and slid the envelope under his blotter.
When he got a free moment, he'd write Alex and tell him how
busy his life had become. Surely he would understand.

What if it had been his own sister, back in Indiana? He tried
to think how he'd feel if she took a notion to move to the city
on her own. With a sigh of resignation, he pulled the envelope
back out and unfolded the letter. Where did Alex say this girl
would be working? He scanned the page.

Southwestern Land and Investments. Mitch sat up at stared
at the paper in his hand. The company belonged to Nathan
Showalter, one of the businessmen he planned to interview. In
fact. . . He shuffled through the papers on his desk. Ah, there it

was. His interview with Showalter was scheduled for tomorrow at eleven.

The tense knot loosened its grip. He could check up on Alex's friend without a bit of trouble. His conscience would be clear, and it would barely make a ripple in his already tight schedule.

four

*More than three hundred days of dazzling sunshine a year and
virtually frost-free winters guarantee the likelihood of two,
or even three, harvests per annum. Water from the mountain
stronghold housing Roosevelt Dam eliminates a dependence on
rainfall, truly making this a paradise for the farmer.*

Catherine read the rest of the clippings on the page, her
excitement mounting with every paragraph. Whoever would
have imagined describing the barrenness of the surrounding
desert in such captivating terms? But the more she read, the
more she could believe in the promise contained in these lines.

Maricopa Farms. She jotted the name down on the list she
had started compiling during the afternoon, marveling at the
varied interests Southwestern controlled. All the different names
had been nothing more than a meaningless hodgepodge at first,
but she was finally beginning to sort them out in her mind.

After spending the day immersed in study, she now had
a sense of the style used in the advertisements, the ways of
phrasing used to show the properties offered in their best light.
By tomorrow, she should be able to pick up where these left
off and write copy that was just as good or maybe even better.

A shadow fell across her desk, and Catherine hunched her
shoulders. *What now, Miss Trautman?* The woman had done
nothing but hover over her all day. *Just like that brindle cow of
Dad's that had to make sure the other cows knew she was the boss.*
Catherine gritted her teeth and kept her eyes focused on the
volume before her. Maybe if she appeared absorbed in her

reading, the woman would go away.

The shadow remained where it was, and Catherine heard a low, masculine cough. She looked up, startled to find a slender, well-dressed man standing on the far side of her desk.

"Good afternoon." A smile lifted the ends of his mustache and crinkled the skin at the corners of his eyes. "I'm Nathan Showalter."

Catherine moved her lips, but no sound came forth. What had she been thinking? Her first day on the job, and she'd just been abominably rude to her new boss. She jumped to her feet. "I'm terribly sorry, I didn't realize. . . ." Her voice trailed off. She dropped her gaze, acutely aware of how foolish she must seem in his eyes.

Mr. Showalter motioned her back to her seat and leaned against the corner of her desk. His smile never dimmed. "I'm glad to see you so absorbed in studying our advertisements. Your job will be of immense importance to this company. But I'm sure you can handle it. Your qualifications looked fine, but I was especially impressed by the way you expressed yourself in your letter. That's exactly the kind of style I was looking for."

Catherine cleared her throat and clasped her hands atop the book to keep him from seeing her fingers tremble. "Mattie told me some of what the company is doing, and I've picked up more details from my reading."

"Good idea. That's an excellent way to prepare yourself." He stepped over to a map that covered a large portion of the adjacent wall, pointing out projects whose names she recognized from her daylong study. "Most of these are in the works. The others are ready to set in motion as soon as we acquire the necessary properties. But they'll happen. It's only a matter of time."

Catherine rose from her desk and stepped over to join him where she could see the map more closely.

"Give us a few years and enough investors, and we can turn this place into a veritable Garden of Eden!" Mr. Showalter tapped the map and gave a self-effacing laugh. "Forgive me for running on so. I'm afraid I let my passion for all this get the best of me."

"No, you're absolutely right." Catherine caught her breath in a quick gasp and gripped her hands together. "What greater opportunity could there be to boost Arizona than to show the rest of the nation the possibilities that exist here?" She glanced up at her boss and saw him staring at her thoughtfully.

She broke off, flustered. "I mean, I'll do my best to portray Southwestern's projects in a most favorable light."

Nathan Showalter nodded slowly. "I'm sure you will. Your enthusiasm is exactly what we need."

ﾞ

"Southwestern Land and Investments has holdings of more than ten thousand acres, did you know that? Oh, of course you did. You've been writing those ads longer than I have." Catherine shoved her trunk up one of the steps at Mrs. Abernathy's boardinghouse while Mattie tugged at the other end.

"It's just amazing, the things that are planned for developing this area." She bumped the heavy trunk up another step and leaned against the wall to catch her breath. "This place is going to be a regular Garden of Eden some day."

She braced her feet on the step and shoved at the trunk again. "Did I tell you Mr. Showalter himself stopped by my desk and spent quite some time telling me about his plans?"

Mattie laughed and pushed a loose strand of hair off her face. "Only about forty times in the last half hour. You've hardly stopped to draw a breath since we left the office."

Together they got behind her cumbersome trunk and heaved it up the final step to the landing. "I'm sorry. It's just that I'm so excited! This job is going to be better than anything I ever imagined." Catherine eyed the distance down the hallway to the room assigned to her. "I've learned so much about the business already, in just one day. We're part of something really big here, Mattie, do you realize that?"

Together the girls pushed the trunk the final few yards down the hall and through the door into Catherine's room.

"What I realize right now," Mattie said, "is that moving that big old case of yours has nearly done me in." Without waiting for an invitation, she flopped across Catherine's bed.

Catherine stopped next to the trunk and surveyed her new home with delight. The room at the Bellmont sported finer appointments, but it had been nothing more than a temporary shelter, and an expensive one at that. This room, though simply furnished, was hers and hers alone.

With her hands on her hips, she turned in a slow circle, then gave a satisfied nod. Plain, but it had potential. A new bedspread, curtains to match, a bright rug on the floor. . . Her imagination took flight before she remembered she was only a tenant here. Perhaps Mrs. Abernathy wouldn't want her changing things to suit herself.

Reality dictated she set the idea aside for the time being, anyway. Redecorating her room, along with refurbishing her wardrobe, would have to wait until she had more funds on hand.

Catherine eyed Mattie, stretched out on the bed and looking like she was ready to drift off to sleep. Every ounce of her being longed to do likewise, but she still needed to unpack and get settled into her new digs.

She lifted the trunk lid and started pulling out the clothes she'd packed so carefully only a few days before. Mattie roused herself enough to sit up and watched with interest while she shook out each garment and slipped it onto a hanger in the wardrobe.

Catherine straightened the sleeve on a green merino dress and slid the hanger along the rod. "It was nice of Mrs. Abernathy to let me move right in. I still can't believe she took me on like that, sight unseen."

"I told you she was wonderful." Mattie reached over to the trunk and fingered the tucks on a white cotton blouse.

Catherine held up her sage green gored skirt and studied it with a critical eye. At home, she'd packed it feeling sure it would fit her needs at work, but after seeing some of the people who came through the office that day, it now struck her as unbearably drab. A pang of inadequacy pierced her excitement. "This is absolutely frumpish."

"No, it isn't," Mattie protested. "It's lovely, and I'm sure it looks very becoming on you."

Catherine hung the skirt over a hook on the wardrobe door and stepped back to view it from a distance. "It won't do, Mattie. It's just plain dowdy. I'm going to have to get a whole set of outfits as soon as I can. I refuse to look like some poor little country mouse!"

Mattie grinned up at her. "With that gorgeous hair of yours, you'd look good in a potato sack."

"It's not only for me," Catherine went on. "What I wear reflects on the company. I need to think of that."

A light tap sounded, and their landlady poked her head around the half-open door. "I just wanted to make sure you were getting settled. Is everything to your liking?"

"Come in, Mrs. Abernathy." Catherine grinned at the little dumpling of a woman who entered the room. Her round face and eyes the color of raisins made Catherine think of one of her mother's currant puddings.

The landlady clasped her hands at her waist and looked at the wardrobe with approval. "My, you're nearly unpacked already." A wave of good cheer radiated from her. "I'm so glad you're going to be part of my household. It will be wonderful to have another Christian young lady staying with me. Is everything to your liking? Is there anything you need?"

"It's perfect, Mrs. Abernathy. Just perfect." Catherine paused and fingered the bedspread. "I was wondering, though. Would you mind if I added a few touches of my own? Not right away, but maybe later on?" She trailed off, hoping she hadn't offended.

Mrs. Abernathy's face split in a pleasant smile. "Suit yourself, dearie. I don't mind a bit. That spread is getting to be a little on the frayed side, come to think of it. And don't worry about hurting my feelings by making suggestions. To my mind, wanting to make the room your own means you're planning to stay a long time. And that's a good thing."

Catherine basked in the woman's friendly glow. "Thank you. I'll plan on picking up a few things as soon as I can afford them."

"I'll be getting back down to the kitchen now," Mrs. Abernathy said. "Supper will be ready in just a bit."

Catherine pulled two blouses from the trunk and held them in front of the green skirt by turns. She shook her head. "Nothing looks right. I need to do something about this."

"What if you pinned a brooch at the neck?" Mattie offered. "I have one you can borrow."

"I don't know if that will be enough to help." Catherine brightened. "You know where the good stores are. Let's plan on going shopping soon."

Mattie lifted one eyebrow. "I thought you were on a tight budget."

Catherine placed the skirt in the wardrobe and shut the door. She gave a rueful laugh. "Well, window-shopping at least."

Mattie giggled with her, and they hurried down to supper.

five

Catherine grabbed up her purse and stuffed a fresh handkerchief inside, then quickly settled her hat on top of her head and gave one last look around the room. *Is there anything I've forgotten?*

She should never have taken the time to try on three different blouses with her green skirt. Those extra minutes spent trying to decide which combination worked best were going to make her late, and she couldn't afford that—not on her second morning at work.

A quick glance in the mirror told her the additional effort had been worth it. The sparkling white blouse with crisp tucks up the front flattered both her face and figure. Mattie's brooch pinned at the neck provided the perfect finishing touch. It wouldn't be up to Miss Trautman's standards by any means, but a definite improvement over the outfit she'd worn the day before.

Looking her best wouldn't make up for being late, though. She hurried down the hallway to Mattie's room and rapped on the door. "Are you ready to leave? Hurry up, or we'll be late."

Her conscience smote her at the implication Mattie might be responsible for her own tardiness. Still, time was ticking away. She was surprised Mattie hadn't been the one to come looking for her long before this.

She didn't leave without me, did she? Panic knotted her stomach, but she dismissed the notion on second thought. She'd only known Mattie a short time but couldn't believe she would do something like that.

Catherine knocked again, harder this time. "Mattie, are you in there?" Worry edged her voice. "It's time to go. We'll have to run to make it, as it is."

She pressed her ear against the door panel and heard a faint groan. Frowning, Catherine turned the knob and pushed the door open a few inches.

Mattie lay curled under her blankets, damp strands of brown hair straggling across her forehead. Catherine pushed the door open wide and started toward the bed.

Mattie waved her back with a feeble gesture. "Don't come close. I don't want you to catch this, whatever it is." She pressed her hand against her mouth to stifle a ragged cough. "Tell Miss Trautman I'm too sick to come to work today, will you? And would you ask Mrs. Abernathy if she'd mind bringing me a cup of tea?"

"You poor thing!" Catherine shifted from one foot to the other. She glanced at the door then back at Mattie. "I wish I could stay and help. Is there anything. . . ? I'll go get Mrs. Abernathy."

The landlady stood with her hands in a sinkful of suds. She looked up and smiled when Catherine clattered into the room.

"Did you oversleep on your first morning here? I wondered, when you missed breakfast."

"Mrs. Abernathy—"

"No, don't apologize. You haven't time for that." She pointed to a paper sack on the counter top. "I've bagged up some biscuits for you to take with you. You can keep them in your desk drawer and snack on them when you get the chance."

"But Mrs. Abernathy—"

The cheerful woman thrust a second bag at her. "And take this one for Mattie. That way she won't have to take time to come get it herself."

"That's just it. Mattie's not going to work. She's sick."

Mrs. Abernathy's lips rounded in dismay. "Sick! The poor lamb."

"She asked me to see if you'd take her a cup of tea. I'd stay and carry it up for you, but I'm in a frightful hurry, and—"

"Of course, of course." Mrs. Abernathy sprang into action, setting the teakettle on a stove burner with one hand and making shooing motions at Catherine with the other. "I'll take care of our Mattie; don't you worry about that. You run along, now. It wouldn't do for you to lose your job almost before you've begun."

She herded Catherine toward the front door, then bustled up the stairs, clucking like a mother hen fussing over her only chick.

Relieved that Mattie was in good hands, Catherine glanced at the hall clock, gasped, and bolted out the door.

❧

"Mattie won't be in to work today, Miss Trautman. She's terribly ill."

The supervisor drew herself up and peered over her spectacles at Catherine. "How could she think of getting sick at a time like this? Doesn't she realize how busy we are? Everyone must carry their share of the load."

I hardly think she took sick just to make things difficult for you. Catherine clamped her tongue between her teeth to keep from speaking the thought aloud.

"I can't possibly be expected to take on more than my own responsibilities right now. And the other girls have plenty to do at their typewriters. It's thoughtless; that's what it is." She eyed Catherine with a dubious expression then seemed to come to a decision. "You will have to take over Mattie's duties for today at least." She clapped her hands briskly. "Go get your things. You can bring them out here and do your work at the reception desk."

"But I—"

Miss Trautman fixed her with a cold stare. "Yes?"

"I'll just get my things and be right there."

❦

With its sweeping vistas and pristine air, the area near Castle Hot Springs lightens the visitor's spirit upon arrival. The soothing waters and dry climate rival any spa to be found in Europe.

Catherine pressed the blotter over the words she had just penned. Would the piece be up to Mr. Showalter's standards? She read the paragraph again.

It had to be. If she couldn't meet her employer's expectation, she might lose her job. Could she bear it if she couldn't measure up and wound up going home in defeat? *That won't happen. God opened up the way for me to be here, and no one is going to run me off.*

"Catherine?" Miss Trautman's piercing voice preceded her down the hallway. "Be sure to show Mr. Westfall in as soon as he arrives. Mr. Showalter is most anxious to speak with him." She paused before turning back to her own office. "And see that you're on your best behavior. He is an important investor. Very important."

Catherine wrinkled her nose at Miss Trautman's retreating back, then rearranged her features as the front door swung open and a rotund gentleman stepped inside.

"I'm Westfall," he announced without preamble. "Is Showalter ready to see me?"

Catherine led the way back to her employer's private office, hoping her demeanor would merit Miss Trautman's approval. Inwardly, she giggled. *He looks like he has plenty to invest, all right. He's certainly well fed.*

Back at the desk, she took advantage of the moment alone

to fluff her hair and smooth the curls hanging down the back of her neck. The idea of trying to please Miss Trautman might rankle, but she recognized the truth that she was the first person at Southwestern to be seen by visitors and thus bore the responsibility for making a good initial impression.

She returned to her work and lost herself in writing descriptions of the sanitarium the company planned to build north of the city. Sometime later, Mr. Westfall breezed back by her desk on his way out, and she glanced up at the clock on the wall behind her, surprised to see how much time had passed. It was almost eleven. *Isn't Mr. Showalter supposed to be meeting with someone else in a few minutes?* She ran her finger down the entries in the appointment book.

Yes, there it was: Mitchell Brewer was scheduled for eleven o'clock. But where was he? The other visitors had been punctual, sometimes arriving several minutes in advance of the appointed hour.

Another minute or two passed. Catherine fidgeted with the papers on her desk. What was she supposed to do if Mr. Brewer didn't appear? Should she notify Mr. Showalter that his appointment hadn't shown up or just stay at her desk and keep on working? Mattie's job wasn't nearly as easy as it seemed on the surface.

❧

Almost eleven o'clock. Mitch picked up his pace and strode east along Jefferson Street. The Southwestern Land and Investments building should be just ahead in the next block. Time for his interview with Nathan Showalter and then to see about taking care of Alex Bradley's request.

That little task might turn out to be easier said than done. It seemed so simple at first. Then he started thinking about just how he planned to go about it. He could hardly go in as a total stranger, ask for Catherine O'Roarke at the front desk, and expect them to produce her, could he?

What reason could he give for asking to see her? He came up with several ideas and scrapped them all. And when he stood face to face with her—assuming he got to see her at all—how could he possibly introduce himself without using Alex's name?

What did I set myself up for this time, Lord? Of all the hare-brained schemes! How do I get myself into these things, anyway? He waited for an answer, but none came.

Mitch stepped off the curb, only to leap back out of the street when he heard a strident *ah-oo-gah!* A Ford runabout sped past only inches away.

Startled out of his woolgathering, Mitch glanced around and realized he had walked a half block too far.

He retraced his steps, hurrying when he heard a clock begin to chime eleven. Trotting up Southwestern's front steps, he realized he didn't have any more idea of how to locate Miss O'Roarke than he did a few moments before.

He pushed the glass door open and swept his hat off in the same motion. Smoothing his hair with one hand, he glanced at the clock hanging over the reception desk.

Barely a minute past the hour. Not as punctual as he'd like to be but not too bad considering his absentminded detour. His gaze shifted to the copper-haired young woman seated behind the desk.

Her lips curved in an inquiring smile. Mitch simply stared, his own lips curving in response.

The receptionist tilted her head and looked at him curiously. "May I help you?"

Mitch recovered his equilibrium enough to stride to the desk, hoping he hadn't lost credibility as a serious journalist. "I'm Mitchell Brewer. Mr. Showalter is expecting me."

Her blue-green eyes sparkled. "You have the eleven o'clock

appointment, then. Please come with me. I'll take you back to Mr. Showalter's office."

Mitch followed along behind her, noting the way her hair changed color when she stepped into the shadows. With the sunlight pouring through the front window and glinting off her curls, the effect made him think of a new penny. Back here in the hallway, it appeared to be more of a strawberry blond.

He couldn't decide which shade appealed to him more, but he had no trouble approving of the way the curls followed the lines of her neck and spilled over her shoulder. Her trim figure moved along with a free, easy stride.

They passed through a small anteroom then stopped outside a closed door. His charming guide tapped on the door, then pushed it open.

"Mr. Brewer is here." She flashed Mitch a smile and stepped back to allow him to enter. Mitch felt his throat go dry. The scent of lilacs filled his nostrils when he brushed past her.

Nathan Showalter rose from his seat behind the massive walnut desk and extended his hand. "Brewer, it's good to meet you." He glanced over Mitch's shoulder. "By the way, Miss O'Roarke, that was a very nice piece you wrote. Keep up the good work." A delighted smile lit the receptionist's face before she closed the door and left them.

Mitch reached out to take Showalter's outstretched hand. While one part of his mind sized up his host, another registered Showalter's words to the receptionist. *Miss O'Roarke? Then that must be. . .* He pulled his attention back to the interview. Business before pleasure, and talking to Catherine O'Roarke would definitely be a pleasure.

ᨑ

"The future belongs to those who are willing to grasp the dream and make it become a reality."

Mitch nodded and jotted down the main points of Showalter's statement. He had already made quick notes summing up the man's appearance, the feel of his handshake, the details that would convey the sum of the man to his readers back East.

"Let me show you what I mean." Showalter stepped across to the far wall and pulled down a map showing Phoenix and its environs. "For years, this area suffered through alternate periods of flood and drought. What we needed was a way to provide water on a steady, manageable basis instead of having either feast or famine. That is exactly what the Roosevelt Dam does.

"And that, Mr. Brewer, is going to turn Phoenix into a Utopia. Look here." He pointed to a spot some distance north of the city. "Do you realize how many people have come to Arizona for their health? We have found the perfect spot to build a sanitarium that will allow them to rest and rejuvenate in the most healthful setting imaginable."

Mitch set his notepad aside and moved to join him. He bent forward for a closer look. "Why, this place is miles from town. There's nothing there but desert."

"Desert today; paradise tomorrow." Showalter clapped Mitch on the shoulder and resumed his seat. He leaned across his desk with an openness that drew Mitch in to his contagious excitement. "Phoenix is growing, Brewer. And this is while we're still a territory. As soon as Taft signs that proclamation of statehood, there's no limit to the growth we'll see.

"We need men of vision, men of purpose to set the stage for maximum potential." He tented his fingers, and his voice took on a pedantic tone. "Change is inevitable, but the kind of change that occurs is open to question. Growth can be allowed to happen on its own, willy-nilly. . .or a guiding hand in the background can steer it in the right direction."

Mitch glanced up from his note taking. "And that hand would belong to. . ."

Showalter smiled. "My intent is to help Arizona develop in a way that all of us can be proud of." He pointed to an easel holding an artist's rendition of the proposed sanitarium. "Let me show you what I mean."

❧

. . .at sunset, when a myriad of colors from the divine Artist's brush paint the entire sky.

Catherine stared at the line, then crossed it out with heavy strokes of her pen. She cradled her forehead in the palm of her hand. What a pathetic effort! A child could do as well—maybe better. What happened to the effortless turn of phrase Mr. Showalter had praised only a short time before? Now, no matter how hard she tried, the words simply wouldn't come. She couldn't think of a coherent sentence to depict the glories of an Arizona sunset.

But she could have described Mitchell Brewer's face without a moment's pause.

His image filled her mind: that unusual combination of brown hair and gray eyes, the smile that made her insides feel like melted butter. . . *Stop it!*

She yanked open her desk drawer and jerked out a fresh sheet of paper. *What is the matter with you, Catherine Elizabeth O'Roarke? If you can't concentrate on your work, you'll lose this job.*

That settled her down in a hurry. She couldn't afford to wait for inspiration; she had to focus her mind on the task at hand and write. Otherwise. . .the specter of returning home a failure would prove to be no specter at all but grim reality.

No. She would not go home in defeat, not after her brave pronouncements. She needed to fix her attention firmly on the task at hand. Her job, that was the important thing, her whole reason for coming here.

Smoothing the sheet of paper, she dipped her pen in the inkwell. She had prayed for this chance, and she wasn't about to miss out on it just because some melting gray eyes gave her goose bumps that would outdo any love-struck schoolgirl's. She had a purpose in life, a mission, and she wouldn't let Mitchell Brewer—or any other man—distract her from her goal.

six

Mitch closed the door of Nathan Showalter's office behind him and stood in the quiet of the empty anteroom. After all the grand notions that had been thrown at him over the past half hour, he needed a moment to collect his thoughts.

If only half of what Showalter talked about came to pass, it meant a greater potential for Arizona than he had ever dreamed possible.

The ideas Showalter presented chased each other around inside Mitch's head. Instead of insubstantial drawings, he could almost see the finished structures already in place. He shook his head. Few men had Showalter's gift for painting a picture with words. Now if he could only do as good a job for the readers of the profile he would write.

He looked around to get his bearings, then started toward the outer office, formulating his opening sentence in his mind. Retracing his steps would take him by the reception desk and then—

He stopped in midstride. *Catherine O'Roarke.* He'd almost forgotten.

For a moment, he considered hustling back to his office before any of his thoughts were lost. Then his conscience prodded him. He had given his word to Alex, and he intended to live up to it.

Ah, well. It wouldn't take more than a minute to make good on his promise. He would visit with her a bit, then go on his way, having fulfilled his obligation to Alex.

❧

Catherine heard footsteps approaching down the hallway in

time to pull herself together before Mitch appeared. She wasn't about to sit there looking at him with calf's eyes. By the time he set foot in the reception area, she sat primly, ready to give him no more than a polite acknowledgment as he left.

To her surprise, he stopped directly in front of her desk and smiled as if they were old friends. "Your boss certainly has a way with words."

Catherine unbent enough to give him a brief smile then leaned over her work again.

"This article I'm going to write should be wonderful publicity for Southwestern Land and Investments."

Catherine glanced up and immediately found herself lost in his gaze. How could she ever get any work done if he persisted on staring at her with those smoky gray eyes?

"So you're writing the copy for the new advertisements? May I see?" Without waiting for an answer, he picked up the page she had turned in to Mr. Showalter earlier and scanned it. "Very nice," he said. "Have you been doing this long?"

Catherine couldn't help but flush with pleasure. "Not long. I just started yesterday, as a matter of fact." *And when did the topic of this conversation turn from the company to me?* She shifted in her chair and fiddled with her pen.

"Only yesterday, eh? Have you lived in Phoenix long?"

The goose bumps reappeared on Catherine's arms, but this time they weren't caused by pleasure. Something about this conversation didn't seem right. "No." She drew the word out. "I'm new here."

"Ah, a newcomer to our fair city." He shuffled from one foot to the other. "Are you enjoying it here? No problems getting settled in?"

Catherine nodded politely but kept a wary eye on him. He looked too nice to fit her mental picture of a masher, but this was the city, after all. It wouldn't hurt to be on her guard.

"I'm getting along quite well, thank you." She put a note of finality into her tone. "And now if you'll excuse me, I really need to get back to work."

Judging by the way the tips of his ears reddened, she had succeeded in making her desire to end the conversation clear. "Of course. Don't let me keep you." He pivoted on his heel, grabbed his hat, and hurried out the door.

Catherine cupped her chin in her hands and stared after him, wishing she hadn't been so abrupt. He probably hadn't meant anything by those questions. It was her own inexperience with the way things were done in the city that made her throw up a wall of caution like that. Next time, she wouldn't be so quick to jump to conclusions.

She bit her lower lip and blinked at the sudden sting of tears. After the way she'd just spoken to Mitchell Brewer, there probably wouldn't be a next time.

ᘒ

Mitch dotted the last *i*, set his pen aside, and swept his pile of notes into his top desk drawer. He hadn't felt this energized in a long time. The profile on Nathan Showalter showed promise, even at this rough stage. Given Showalter's gift with words, it hadn't been hard to breathe life into the developer's plans.

He slid the article draft into a folder and pushed it to one side of his desk. At least he'd been able to get the basic shape of the article roughed out while his impressions of Showalter were still fresh in his mind. Now he needed to get back to business for the *Clarion*.

Mitch checked his appointment calendar. Oh, yes. He was supposed to be covering the announcement to add more electric streetcars to the line connecting Phoenix to Glendale. That was supposed to start in. . . He checked his pocket watch. *Oh, brother.* Only ten minutes to go.

He stood and yanked his coat from the back of his chair.

Thrusting his arms into the sleeves while he walked, he hustled toward the door. It seemed like everything in his life was happening at top speed these days. He pushed through the door to the street and hurried along the sidewalk to where he'd parked his roadster. Much as he preferred walking, he would never make it on time otherwise.

He maneuvered the auto down Washington Street, managing to avoid pedestrians and an oncoming motor car while he circled around a horse-drawn wagon. His life had become a similar juggling act, taking every bit of effort just to make sure he got everything done. Even so, he lived with an underlying fear he was going to wake up some day and find out he'd made a royal mess of things. He tooted his horn at a delivery wagon driver who had stopped to pass the time of day with a man standing in front of a café.

Look at the way he'd mixed up the figures in that article on mining production. It was a good thing he caught the error before Dabney saw it. That could have been a real catastrophe.

Mitch had an uneasy feeling he hadn't done so well with his mission for Alex, either. Once he found himself face to face with Catherine O'Roarke, every coherent thought had flown out of his mind and he'd fumbled his words like a schoolboy with stage fright.

Had he sounded as ridiculous to her as he had to himself? He went over the conversation in his mind while he parked the roadster, patted his coat pocket to make sure he had his notepad, and dashed off toward the meeting. Thinking back to what he'd said, he winced. No doubt about it, that little speech wouldn't win him any awards for eloquence.

He skidded in the door just in time to catch the speaker's opening remarks. Whipping out his notepad, he scribbled frantically, trying to keep up with what was being said.

Thoughts of his conversation with Catherine O'Roarke

invaded his mind, distracting him from the job at hand. What had it sounded like from her point of view? He hoped he hadn't come across as though he was trying to be too familiar. The more he thought about it, the more he felt sure he had done just that.

Calm down, Brewer. You did what Alex asked you to and found out what you needed to know. Her opinion of you doesn't really matter.

He grunted, drawing an irritated look from the man standing in front of him. Mitch cleared his throat and tried to look like he was still focused on a meeting that no longer held any importance. To his amazement, he realized that it mattered very much what Catherine O'Roarke thought of him.

◆

"Glad to be back at your own desk?" Enid's blue eyes shone with a friendly light.

Catherine slid into her chair and set her purse inside the bottom drawer. "More than you can imagine." Three days of covering Mattie's post at the front desk had given her a new appreciation of the skills it took to be a successful receptionist.

Thanks to Mrs. Abernathy's tender care and lavish doses of chicken soup and peppermint tea, Mattie had recovered from her ailment, and this Monday morning found her back in her regular place.

Mattie was pleased; Catherine was delighted beyond measure. Dividing her attention between a new prospectus for the sanitarium and the steady stream of callers wanting to speak to Mr. Showalter produced more frayed nerves than usable copy, something Miss Trautman had been quick to point out.

Catherine squared her notes into a neat stack, pulled her pen from the center drawer, and prepared to prove Mr. Showalter hadn't made a mistake in hiring her.

"Did you hear about the group marching for women's rights?" Enid asked. "They're going to rally at the capitol on Saturday."

Irene frowned. "Why get so worked up about it? We'll either get the vote, or we won't. It doesn't really matter to me."

The pen slipped through Catherine's fingers and clattered on her desk. "You can't mean that!" She shoved her chair backward and bounced to her feet.

Enid and Irene stared openmouthed.

Irene lifted one shoulder in a tentative shrug. "I can voice my opinion at home all I want, but my dad and my brothers are the ones who'll have the final say. What difference will one vote make? It's a man's world. It always has been."

"But it doesn't have to stay that way." Catherine's breath came quickly, and she knew from the burning in her cheeks that her face must be turning red. "Do you realize the lengths women before us have gone to in order to assure us of having a voice in government? Do you have any idea of the sacrifices they have made?"

Enid and Irene glanced at each other then shook their heads slowly.

Emboldened, Catherine stepped in front of their desks and struck a pose. "Listen, both of you. A woman's mind is every bit the equal of a man's—sometimes better, if you ask me."

A voice behind her made her jump. "But no one asked you, did they, Miss O'Roarke?"

Enid gasped, and Irene turned pale. Both girls ducked their heads and focused all their attention on the papers before them.

Catherine felt a crawling sensation along her spine, like the time Alex Bradley dumped a handful of grasshoppers down her neck. Gathering what dignity she could muster, she tilted her chin and turned to face Miss Trautman.

"We were only discussing the rights of women."

The supervisor narrowed her eyes. "You are not being paid to discuss politics. Nor are you being paid to waste the time of the other employees. Mr. Showalter will not put up with such goings-on. You are being paid—in case you have forgotten—to write copy for advertisements for the benefit of Southwestern Land and Investments. . .something you have found trouble doing ever since you arrived."

Catherine opened her mouth to make a retort then clamped her lips shut. All she would accomplish by arguing was to receive another reprimand. . .or maybe a dismissal. That prospect didn't bear thinking about.

She forced a tight smile and bobbed her head. "Yes, ma'am." She returned to her chair and bent over her work. She could feel Miss Trautman's icy stare lingering on her for several long moments before she heard the supervisor's footsteps clicking their way down the short hallway to her own office.

"Whew." Irene let out her breath in a *whoosh*. "That Trautman is a cold fish, all right."

Both the other girls giggled, and Catherine felt some of her tension slip away. She hadn't said anything wrong; she'd just chosen the wrong time to say it. If Irene and Enid were truly interested in learning more about the importance of suffrage, maybe she could set a time after work for the three of them to discuss the matter away from Miss Trautman's keen ears.

Silence settled over the room, broken only by the tap of typewriter keys and the scratching of Catherine's pen nib across her paper.

An oasis in the desert, she wrote, remembering Mr. Showalter's glowing description. *The Phoenix area is destined to replace the likes of Baden Baden as—*

"Catherine?"

—the premier destination for those seeking healing for the body

and balm for the soul. The salubrious climate and—

"Catherine!" Irene's sharp whisper pierced the stillness.

"What is it?" Jolted from her concentration, her tone sounded sharper than she intended.

"I just wondered—do you really think women should be involved in politics?"

"Of course. How else can we affect society? You said it's a man's world. Well, maybe that is what's wrong with it."

Irene shot a furtive glance toward the door and lowered her voice even more. "I'm only working here until I find a husband. How can a woman fulfill her role in the home if she's going out and stirring things up?"

"How can she be sure she will have a home to run if she leaves control of her life in men's hands?" Honestly, didn't these women ever think about anything beyond snaring a husband and the seeming security that brought? Catherine laid down her pen and crossed the distance between their desks.

Irene's lips formed an O. "I never thought about it that way."

"Well, you should."

The door behind Catherine squeaked, and she whirled around. Mattie stood in the doorway. "What on earth are you carrying on about? If Miss Trautman hears you—"

"She won't if you keep your voice down," Irene shot back. "Let Catherine talk. This is starting to make sense."

"It makes perfect sense," Catherine went on, buoyed by their interest. "This isn't just the whim of a few radical individuals. Women have fought long and hard to reach this moment in history, and we don't dare turn back when we're on the brink of victory."

Her audience stared at her, eyes shining. "Is it possible, then?" Enid whispered. "Is suffrage for women really that close?"

"It is if we don't give up. Imagine how wonderful it will be if Arizona celebrates this momentous step in her history by allowing women the right to vote!"

She raised her right arm in a sweeping gesture and glanced at the others in anticipation of a quiet round of applause.

Irene's and Enid's mouths hung open. Both girls stared at a point over Catherine's left shoulder, then dropped their gazes to their desks and started typing furiously.

A sinking feeling buzzed in the pit of Catherine's stomach. Miss Trautman. It had to be. She squared her shoulders and took a deep breath, hoping she could brazen out another rebuke. With her head held high, she turned. . .and looked straight into the face of Nathan Showalter.

"Would you come with me, please?" Without waiting for a reply, he turned on his heel and strode down the hallway toward his office.

Catherine waited for the floor to open and swallow her up. When it didn't, she forced her feet to follow in his wake. Just past the door, Miss Trautman stood, arms folded across her chest and a smug expression in her eyes.

It took all the courage Catherine could muster to tilt her chin and stride past without a break in her step. She might be about to lose her coveted job, but she refused to give her supervisor the satisfaction of seeing her mortification.

Before she rounded the corner, she darted a quick glance over her shoulder. Mattie still stood rooted near the doorway as though turned to stone. Her look of sympathy confirmed Catherine's fears. Mattie, too, knew she was about to be sacked.

Mr. Showalter stood behind his desk and gestured toward a chair. Catherine sank into it gratefully. Her legs wouldn't have held her upright another moment. She crossed her ankles and folded her hands loosely in her lap, trying to maintain the appearance of dignified calm. Inside, she felt like a whimpering child.

The last time she'd felt so disgraced had been at age ten, the time her father caught her trying out some language she'd learned from a cowboy he'd recently hired. The results of today's offense would be even more painful, and both times it was the fault of her own willful nature.

Mr. Showalter settled into his heavy chair and cleared his throat. Catherine braced herself.

"That was quite a performance you put on out there."

Catherine nodded miserably, not trusting herself to speak. Even worse than being taken to task like this would be the humiliation of breaking down in front of her employer.

Mr. Showalter leaned back and rocked his chair, studying her intently. Catherine wanted to scream at him to go on and get it over with. She twisted her fingers together until they ached.

"You strike me as a rather opinionated young woman, Miss O'Roarke."

Catherine swallowed hard and prayed her voice wouldn't crack. "I've been told that before." She offered him a weak smile.

"Your views on women's suffrage, for instance." He tented his fingers and tapped his thumbs together.

Here it came. Catherine drew a slow breath and waited for the axe to fall. Would an apology do anything to ward off the blow?

"I happen to subscribe to that view myself."

"I'm sorry. I know my tongue runs away with me sometimes and. . . You do?"

Mr. Showalter chuckled. "I knew from your first day here I hadn't hired a run-of-the-mill worker."

Not knowing what to say, Catherine held her tongue for once.

"Your enthusiasm for statehood, your knowledge of current affairs, and your willingness to speak out on issues you feel passionately about. . .hardly what I'd expect to find in this office."

Catherine closed her eyes. Now he would tell her he had no choice but to let her go.

"I must say I appreciate your candor and your ability to express yourself."

Catherine's eyes flew open. Had she heard him correctly? Her hands gripped the arms of her chair.

Mr. Showalter didn't seem to notice. "Irene and Enid are quite capable of keeping up with the regular correspondence. They do a fine job of that. However. . ." He leaned forward, and the smile faded from his face. "I have correspondence of a sensitive nature, delicate negotiations I'd rather not send through the normal office channels."

Catherine nodded, though she didn't have the least idea what he could be talking about.

"I've been thinking for some time that I need someone to work closely with me, someone who understands the importance of this moment in Arizona's history and has the vision to appreciate it." He regarded her steadily. "So what do you think?"

Catherine stopped nodding and stared. "About what?"

Mr. Showalter threw back his head and laughed. "I'm offering you a job as my private secretary. Are you interested in the position?"

"Am I?" Catherine held back a whoop. "But I've only been here a short time. Surely Enid or Irene—"

"I said they were capable, but that's as far as it goes. They're quite adequate for the work they're doing, but this position requires something more. With them, the mission of Southwestern Land and Investments is just a job; with you, it's a passion."

"Yes, but—"

"I can have the anteroom just outside fixed up so you'll have a place of your own. It will give you more privacy, and you'll be the one to deal with the people who come to meet with me. Would that suit you?"

"Oh, it would suit me just fine. I mean, yes, sir. Thank you, Mr. Showalter. Thank you very much." She rose and floated toward the door.

His voice stopped her. "The promotion comes with a raise in pay, of course."

It was all she could do to keep from skipping her way back to her desk. Her *former* desk, she reminded herself gleefully.

Inside the office, Enid and Irene sent swift glances her way, but their fingers didn't stop their rapid *rat-tat-tat* on the typewriter keys. Catherine grimaced. They'd probably gotten an earful from Miss Trautman and didn't want to risk being tarred with the same brush as she.

Taken by a sudden fit of impishness, she slowed her steps and heaved a great sigh. From the corner of her eye, she could see Enid's shoulders tense.

Catherine plopped into her chair and sighed again, then pulled open her desk drawers and began removing her personal effects. The rattle of typewriter keys didn't slacken, but she heard a sniffle from Enid's direction.

The door to the front office squeaked on its hinges, and Mattie stepped through the doorway, clutching a sodden handkerchief. Footsteps clicked along the hallway behind Mattie, and Miss Trautman appeared, a knowing smirk on her face. Catherine assumed the most subdued expression she could, then stood and gathered her things.

"I'm leaving now," she said to the room in general. The typists' fingers stilled at last. Everyone looked straight at her.

"I've enjoyed working with you," she went on. That held true for Mattie, Enid, and Irene at any rate.

Mattie stifled a sob. "I'm so sorry, Catherine. Wherever will you go?"

Catherine tossed her head and grinned. "Why, down the hall to my new office. Mr. Showalter just made me his private secretary."

Silence gripped the room for a moment. Then Miss Trautman uttered a strangled cry. Her face paled and her mouth worked, but no words came forth. Directing a baleful glare at Catherine, she pivoted on her heel and stormed down the hallway toward her own office.

Enid, Irene, and Mattie broke into cheers, and Mattie rushed to hug her. "That's wonderful news. We thought. . . well, we thought—"

Catherine returned her hug. "I know what you thought. Will you forgive me for momentarily deceiving you?"

"I'll think about it," Mattie said, giving her a playful swat on the arm. "At the moment, I'd much rather give you a good shake for scaring us all like that."

seven

Arizona is ready to move into a new era. John Murphy,
Edmund Garner, and Nathan Showalter are the vanguard of
those ready to lead her there.

Mitch studied the final line of his article's rough draft. His
stomach twinged, and he pressed his palm flat against his
midsection. He'd done that more than once this afternoon. Maybe
it was the fried chicken he'd picked up for lunch at Felson's Diner.

Or maybe it was guilt gnawing a hole in his middle.

Integrity—hadn't that been his watchword? And he'd blithely
tossed it aside in misleading Catherine O'Roarke about his
interest in talking to her. It might have been more an omission
of the whole truth than an outright lie, but the result was the
same: He hadn't been completely honest with her.

The memory of her pleasant look turning to one of wariness
haunted him. What if he'd frightened her, turned her grand
adventure in Phoenix to one of unnecessary caution and
mistrust?

But it wouldn't hurt for her to be watchful. This was the city,
after all. A young girl needed to develop a degree of caution.
He might have done her a favor by putting her on her guard.

Sure he had.

He shoved the papers on his desk into an untidy heap and
grabbed his jacket.

One of the copyboys hustled over to his desk. "Mr. Dabney
wants to know if you've finished that piece on the body they
found in the canal."

"Tell him I'll have it for him before we go to press. I'm heading over to Southwestern Land and Investments." He left the lad standing there, gaping.

Mitch took a moment at the foot of the steps outside the Southwestern building to catch his breath and straighten his tie. A few extra details from Nathan Showalter would help flesh out his article. He could use that as his excuse for showing up at Miss O'Roarke's desk unannounced.

Making excuses again? The thought chafed at him. The profile on Showalter would be solid enough without additional information.

But it was a credible—and honest—reason for being there. More detail would surely make the piece stronger. He needed a way to get his foot in the door so he'd have a chance to explain his main motive in coming.

How he would do that still remained a problem. He'd rehearsed several opening lines on the way over but couldn't find one that sounded reasonable.

Mitch pulled his handkerchief from his pocket and wiped his moist palms. Heavy clouds draped the sky and obscured the sun. The dismal day seemed a perfect reflection of his own mood. This felt like the first visit all over again. Was he crazy for doing this?

Maybe. But he couldn't live with himself until he straightened out the mess he'd created.

"Looks like you're just going to have to jump right in and take whatever comes, Brewer." He tucked his handkerchief back in place and trotted up the steps.

Once inside, his glance went immediately to the reception desk. A diminutive brown-haired woman gave him a cheerful smile.

"Good afternoon, sir. May I help you?"

Mitch halted in midstride. The greeting he had planned died on his lips. What now?

Should he turn around and leave? His hand groped for the doorknob. No, he couldn't. He'd come this far already; he could at least talk to Showalter, make this a legitimate business call.

"I'd like to speak to Mr. Showalter, if I may."

The receptionist consulted a book on her desk. "Do you have an appointment?"

"No." Mitch pulled at his collar. "I was just in the neighborhood and thought I'd pop in and see if he's available." Inwardly, he groaned. If that didn't sound like an idiotic idea!

From the look on the receptionist's face, she thought so, too. "Mr. Showalter is a very busy man, but I'll see if he can spare you a few moments. What is your name?"

"Brewer. Mitchell Brewer. I spoke to him last week."

The receptionist paused in the archway. "Brewer?" She grinned. "Wait here. I'll see what I can do."

Mitch shuffled his feet on the hardwood floor and wished he'd never thought up this fool venture. Without the sunlight pouring in through the windows, the office seemed dimmer than he remembered. He had a sudden urge to bolt out the door and get some fresh air.

A moment later, the brown-haired receptionist returned. "Mr. Showalter is in conference; perhaps his secretary can help you." She gestured to the archway behind her.

Catherine O'Roarke stepped around the corner and smiled. "Good afternoon, Mr. Brewer. How nice to see you again."

Outside, the clouds still hung heavy. Inside, the sun came out, and light flooded the room. Mitch grinned at his flight of fancy, even as he warmed to the sight of Catherine. A smiling Catherine, no less.

He smiled back but didn't say a word. He didn't need to. Some sort of connection had just established itself between them, one that rendered speech unnecessary. He felt as if he could gaze at her forever, knowing she would understand his every thought.

The receptionist cleared her throat. "Don't mind me. I'll just fade back into the woodwork and leave you two alone. Pretend I'm not here."

Catherine's cheeks turned bright pink, and she glanced around as if wondering what she was doing.

"Thank you, Mattie," she said and looked back at Mitch with laughter dancing in those marvelous blue-green eyes.

Mitch tilted his head. Would you call her eyes turquoise? Or robin's-egg blue? Maybe aquamarine. It would take study—lots of study. And he was more than ready to volunteer his time to the effort.

"I'm sorry," Catherine said, "but Mr. Showalter is meeting with some investors. Is there anything I can do to help?"

Marry me. Mitch shoved his hands in his pockets. "I just needed to check a couple of facts, make sure all the details are correct before I send my story in."

"Perhaps I can find the information for you." She gestured toward the hallway. "Would you care to come back to my office?"

Would he! He trailed behind her eagerly, barely noticing Mattie's quiet snicker on his way out.

Catherine led the way to the anteroom Mitch remembered just outside Nathan Showalter's office. But what a difference! Last time he visited, the room had been empty save for a single wooden chair. Today he saw a cozy nook holding a tiny desk, a row of filing cabinets, and a trailing plant. In only a few days, Catherine had turned the vacant area into a warm, welcoming place.

The same way she'd begun to fill the void in Mitch's heart. *Whoa, there, Brewer.* He shook his head to clear it. *You're just here to set things straight. Better get a rein on that imagination of yours.*

Catherine swept around the small desk with a fluid motion that reminded him of a graceful deer. She leaned against the corner of the desk and looked at him expectantly.

For the life of him, Mitch couldn't remember what he'd planned to say. So he contented himself with staring at Catherine O'Roarke.

She held his gaze, and her lips curved in a gentle smile. Time no longer existed; only the two of them in this moment.

Catherine folded her arms and tipped her head to one side. "You said you had some questions?"

Mitch felt like he had been called back from a far distance. He nodded. "Just a couple."

Another pause. "And those would be?" Catherine prompted.

Mitch's gaze didn't waver from her face. "I. . .wanted to check on when he planned to break ground for the new sanitarium. There was something else. I'll remember it in a minute."

Catherine nodded slowly, seeming no more inclined than he to break the tender mood. She riffled through a stack of papers on her desk. "Here it is. The ground breaking is scheduled for next April." She held the paper out to Mitch.

His fingers touched hers when he reached for it, and he froze. For a long moment neither of them moved.

He glanced down at their fingertips, fully expecting to see sparks shooting back and forth between them like sparklers on the Fourth of July. When he didn't, he looked back up at Catherine and managed a small grin. "I guess I ought to leave. You need to get back to work."

She blinked like a person waking up from a dream. "Yes. Yes, I do."

Still, neither of them moved. Mitch longed to stretch his fingers out a few more inches and wrap her delicate hand in his. He started to act on his desire then remembered where he was.

He shifted his weight. Pleasant as it might be, standing here feeling like he'd found his soul mate wasn't the reason he had come. Nathan Showalter's meeting, just on the other side of the connecting door, could end at any moment and cut off further conversation with Catherine.

"I need to tell you something." His voice came out in a hoarse rasp. He cleared his throat and tried again. "About the other day, when I was in here. I'm afraid I left you with a bad impression. I felt like I came across as some kind of predator."

"Oh, no!" Catherine's eyes widened; then she smiled. "Well, maybe a little."

"I'm sorry about that. I guess I wasn't acting like myself because I wasn't being completely aboveboard with you."

Catherine's forehead crinkled. "What do you mean?"

"The truth is, I'm a friend of Alex Bradley's. He asked me to—"

"Check up on me?" A wry smile twisted her lips.

"No. Well. . .maybe a little." Mitch grinned. "He just wanted to find out how you're doing."

"So all this—the visit, this conversation—was set up for my benefit?"

What happened to the tender look of a moment before? Right now, her eyes were sparking like blue-green flame.

"Not at all. The profile I'm writing is legitimate. I arranged for the interview before I ever knew you worked here. When Alex wrote to ask me to look you up and said you had a job here, I decided I could kill two birds with one stone. I figured it was just a lucky break for me." His voice thickened. "A very lucky break."

Catherine's lashes lowered and hid her gaze from him. Mitch watched her intently. She looked up at last and smiled. His heart warmed. "So you forgive me?"

She studied him for a long moment then nodded. "You are most definitely forgiven, Mitchell Brewer." She tilted her head to one side. "How do you know Alex?"

"He and his father came down to Phoenix for a meeting of the Arizona Cattle Grower's Association a few years back. I was covering the meeting and noticed him reading a copy of *The House of a Thousand Candles* during one of the breaks."

Catherine laughed, a sound Mitch decided he'd like to hear again and again. "That's Alex, all right, forever with his nose in a book."

"I'm afraid I have to plead guilty to the same habit. We talked about the book over lunch and found out we hit it off pretty well. We've kept in touch ever since. Alex is a great fellow. But I'm sure you know that already, having grown up with him."

A tiny dimple appeared in Catherine's cheek. "I wouldn't always have agreed with that, but you're right; he's a pretty special person. It's too bad he never mentioned you."

"I was just thinking the same thing." An idea flitted into his mind. "Would you care to come to church with me this Sunday? We could go out for lunch afterward."

He saw the guarded look return to Catherine's eyes and wanted to kick himself for moving too fast. He hastened to explain. "Several of my friends—a mixed group—generally get together for lunch after the worship service. We could join them so it wouldn't be just the two of us."

She hesitated long enough to make him wish he'd held his tongue. Then her face lit up. "I'd like that," she said simply.

The door behind Catherine swung open, and a heavyset man emerged. Nathan Showalter followed, looking surprised but pleased when he spotted Mitch.

"You've made a wise choice, Bill," he said to his departing visitor. "You won't regret investing with Southwestern. Let me know if you'd like to venture further with us."

When the other man left, Showalter turned to Mitch. "Nice to see you, Brewer. What can I do for you today?"

"I needed some information, but Catherine. . .your secretary. . . already got it for me."

Showalter glanced between the two of them. "I see. Is there anything else I can do for you?"

Mitch picked up his hat and threw one more look at Catherine. "Thanks, but I believe I have everything I need."

eight

"Look at that gorgeous taffeta." Mattie pressed her face so near the front window of M. Goldwater and Bro.'s department store that a puff of steam appeared on the glass. "You'd look a treat in that aqua dress, Catherine. The lavender, too."

Catherine stared at the lavish confections and caught her breath. Both were stunning. Both were stylish. And both were well beyond her means.

"I may have gotten a raise, but I still have rent to pay and meals to buy. I can't spend it all on new clothes."

"How about part of it, then? You're always talking about needing something new, and these are so beautiful. See, they're having a sale. Let's at least go in and look."

"I shouldn't." Catherine eyed the notice in the window. "But I'm going to."

Inside the store, she stared at the modish apparel on display. Truth to tell, it hadn't taken much for Mattie to persuade her to come inside. She'd spent enough time over the past week staring longingly at Goldwaters' ads in the *Arizona Republican* to be able to recite most of their inventory from memory. It would be fun to see firsthand what they had to offer.

Reality surpassed even the most effusive descriptions in the ads and served to underscore the contrast between her own garb and what well-dressed Phoenix women wore. The decision didn't require conscious thought: She couldn't leave the store empty-handed.

She fingered the delicate fabrics and made some rapid calculations. Thanks to finding Mrs. Abernathy's boardinghouse right away instead of prolonging her stay at the Bellmont, she still had a bit left from when she first arrived. With that, plus the increase in pay as Mr. Showalter's private secretary, she could afford to splurge a little.

With a wistful glance at the taffeta dresses—even at the sale price, they were still out of reach—she pulled Mattie toward the rear of the store. "Come on. Let's take a look at those street dresses."

Mattie didn't require a second invitation. She followed along eagerly. "That Mitch Brewer is every bit as good-looking as you said he was. I just about died when he walked into the office and gave me his name."

Catherine ducked her head to hide the flush she felt creep up her neck. "Forget about Mitch Brewer for now." She sorted through the dresses on the rack and held up two selections. "I'm not sure which one I like better. What do you think?"

Mattie held one dress at a time against Catherine and studied them with a judicious air. "This light blue one. It brings out the sparkle in your eyes."

"All right. The light blue it shall be." She started to put the other dress back in its place then paused. "This gray is lovely, too, though."

"Hmm. Speaking of eyes, weren't Mitch Brewer's gray?"

Catherine swatted Mattie on the arm. "Stop it!" She broke into a fit of giggles. "Just for that, I won't take the gray dress after all."

"Then how about this pale green number with the tucks down the front?" Mattie correctly interpreted Catherine's gasp as one of pleasure and handed it to her. "And speaking of eyes again, I'd like to see Mitch Brewer's light up when he sees you in that outfit."

"Honestly, Mattie! Just for that, I ought to put this one back, too."

Mattie gave her a saucy wink. "But you won't."

"No. I won't." The two girls laughed and headed for another display.

An hour later, they emerged from the store with Catherine juggling two paper-wrapped bundles containing her new dresses, a deep purple dress skirt with two rows of French braid, and—tucked discreetly at the bottom of the smaller parcel—one of Thomson's glove-fitting corsets, which the saleslady assured Catherine would give her new clothes the smartest possible fit.

"Here, let me take one." Mattie relieved her of the package on top. "I should have stopped you from buying that rose-colored waist for me, but I'll pay you back come payday."

"You'll do no such thing. If it hadn't been for you, I would have spent far more than that on hotel bills with nothing to show for it. Now I have a wonderful place to live as well as a good friend. I'm the one who got the best of the bargain."

"Which one are you going to wear tomorrow?" Mattie's eyes twinkled.

"Hmm. I'm not sure." Catherine let her mind linger on the delicious dilemma. "Maybe I'll wait and save them for a special occasion."

"You mean like the next time Mitch Brewer makes an appointment to see the boss. . .or his secretary?"

Catherine continued south along First Street. "Hardly. I was just going along with your silliness. I shouldn't be thinking about Mitch Brewer at all right now." She stopped at the corner of Washington. "I'm here to do a job, and I need to keep my mind on business."

Spotting a break in traffic, she dashed across Washington. "I really don't have time to be daydreaming about some man."

Mattie hopped up on the curb beside her. Pausing to catch her breath, she nodded wisely. "That would explain why you were woolgathering at your desk when I brought those papers back to you this afternoon."

Catherine swatted at her again and nearly dropped the package in her arms. "Now look what you made me do. I almost lost this parcel."

Mattie laughed. "Better a parcel than your heart." She scampered out of arm's reach before Catherine could swing again.

*

Mitch strolled up the steps of Southwestern Land and Investments and entered the reception area with a jaunty air. "Good morning, Mattie. I thought your boss would like to see the way the article I did on him turned out." He waved a copy of a Baltimore newspaper at her.

The dark-haired receptionist grinned up at him. "Do you want to leave it here with me, or is there some reason you'd like to go on back to his office?"

Mitch pulled a bag of lemon drops from his pocket and set it on her desk. Mattie drew herself up with an offended expression. "Do I look like a child you can bribe with candy?" She popped one of the drops in her mouth and winked. "Go on back there. And just for future reference, I like peppermints, too."

"I'll make a note of that." Mitch chuckled and headed down the hallway.

Catherine looked up with a bright smile. "I didn't expect to see you here today."

"I hope you're not disappointed."

Her turquoise eyes assured him of her answer even before she spoke. "Not at all."

Mitch let out a breath he didn't realize he'd been holding and handed her the copy of the article. "I brought this for Mr. Showalter. I thought he'd enjoy seeing the finished product."

"Oh, good. He'll be delighted to read it. Did you need to speak to him?"

"There's no need to bother him. You can give it to him later." He handed her the paper. "Are you busy right now?"

"Not too busy to visit for a few minutes." She came around to the front of her desk and leaned against it.

The scent of lilacs wafted over to him. "Thanks for coming to church with me last week. I enjoyed your company." He took a step nearer, then another. She didn't seem to object.

"I liked the service. Your pastor made some good points in his sermon." She smiled up at him. "Lunch was fun, too. I liked meeting your friends."

Emboldened, he gathered his courage to say, "One of the fellows at the paper told me about a concert Friday night. It sounds like it ought to be well worth hearing. Would you like to go with me?"

The light in her face dimmed. "I'm sorry. I already promised Mr. Showalter I'd work late that evening."

"Oh, I see. That's okay. I just thought I'd check. Let me know what your boss thinks about the article." He sketched a wave and headed down the hallway, barely noticing Mattie's cheery greeting on the way out.

He'd done it again. When would he learn to quit moving too far, too fast?

☙

"I'm going downtown after dinner." Mattie slipped one folder into its place in the filing cabinet and reached for another one. "Woolworth's is having a sale. Want to come with me? It'll be fun."

"Not today. You'll have to go without me this time."

"Oh, come on. You know how wonderful you look in the new clothes you got from Goldwaters'. Even Miss Trautman approves of them, though she'd never admit that to you. And Woolworth's prices are lower. You can afford to pick up another outfit or two."

Catherine shook her head. "I have to work late. I'm not even sure I'll make it home in time for dinner."

Mattie slammed the file drawer shut and stared at Catherine. "You're working late again? What is it this time?"

"Mr. Showalter is meeting with some men after the office closes. He needs me to take notes and look up any information that's needed. You know he can never find what he wants when he needs it."

"Is this the same bunch he met with the last time you stayed late? All those mysterious people you can't tell me about?" Mattie huffed when Catherine evaded her gaze. "This is getting to be a habit. Why doesn't he meet with them during office hours, anyway?"

Catherine adopted a lofty tone. "They're very important people, and they're all quite busy. It's difficult enough to get them all together at the same time. We have to do it when we can."

Mattie folded her arms. "So what are you doing that's so important?"

"Making plans for the future of Arizona, that's what." Catherine grabbed a handful of folders and sorted through them.

"Hmph." Mattie snorted. "I thought that was already being done by the legislature."

Catherine pulled out the folder she needed and sighed. "You don't understand, Mattie. Achieving statehood is just the beginning. I can't give you any details about what's going on, but I can tell you that things are being set in motion that will bring about some great improvements for all of us."

And I'm a part of it. The thought kept dancing in her head. Who cared if she had to work extra hours? Going in early and staying late might seem excessive to Mattie, but it still didn't add up to the kind of hours ranchers kept. And it would all be worth it in the end.

She realized Mattie was speaking again. "What did you say?"

"I said at least we'll have some time together on Sunday. There's a potluck after church, remember?"

"Oh, that's right. I meant to tell you, I won't be going to church this week."

Mattie lifted one eyebrow. "Oh?"

Catherine slid the folder into her top desk drawer, careful to avoid Mattie's sharp gaze. "Mr. Showalter asked me to come in and work on Sunday."

Both of Mattie's eyebrows soared toward her hairline.

Catherine felt herself flush. "He wants to get some extra work done when the office is quiet and no one is around."

She squared the remaining folders into a neat stack, resenting the feeling of being put on the spot like that. It had been hard enough to answer Mitch's concerns when she had told him she couldn't go to church with him. Now she had Mattie to deal with as well.

Mattie planted her right hand on her hip and narrowed her eyes. "Are you sure work is all he has in mind?"

Catherine banged the folders down on the desk. "Quite sure." And it was true. She had no doubts at all about her boss's intentions toward her. Never once had he treated her with anything other than an easy camaraderie. No, her heart wasn't in any jeopardy from Nathan Showalter.

But if she wanted to be honest with herself, she couldn't say the same about Mitch Brewer.

"I don't know," Mattie said. "It just doesn't seem right, working on Sunday."

Catherine looked at her friend and forced a smile. "Don't fuss about it so. I know you and Mitch think it practically makes me a heathen, but missing church one Sunday isn't the end of the world."

nine

Abner Schwartz hooked his thumbs in his vest pockets. "I'll agree that projects like the spa are all well and good, but I'm not at all sure about this resort, the Phoenician. I personally know several men who are getting nervous and are ready to pull out. Frankly, I'm thinking of pulling out, myself."

"Wait a minute." Seth Kincaid stood to face the naysayer. "Roosevelt Dam is giving them the means to do most anything requiring water, including filling the lagoons at the resort. The Phoenician is going to be a sight to behold."

"And don't overlook the proximity to the railroad," added Wiley McDermott. "Why, we can build our own station and bring clients right to our door."

"That's right," Kincaid agreed. "The city is expanding, which will only increase the resort's value. That hundred acres will give us the seclusion and exclusivity our guests require, but they will have greater access to shopping and city amenities."

Catherine sat in the far corner of Nathan Showalter's office, her pen racing across her notepad as she tried to keep up with the spirited discussion.

Abner Schwartz grunted. "We don't have the full hundred acres."

An uneasy silence fell over the room.

Catherine tilted the notepad on her lap and flexed her fingers behind it. Not for anything would she want Mr. Showalter to think her incapable of doing a competent job. Cramped fingers were a trivial price to pay for the privilege of being a small part of history in the making.

Today's gathering, though, lacked the convivial air of previous meetings. She knew something significant was afoot when Mr. Showalter announced he had called a meeting on Sunday afternoon. Sure enough, tension seemed to crackle in the air the moment the group assembled. Catherine half expected lightning bolts to start flashing right there in the room.

Ellis Todd cleared his throat. Catherine picked up her pen, ready to write.

"I have to go along with Abner, here. We've all heard the plans: one hundred acres of prime land to build a resort that will rival anything in the nation. All this talk about a palm-lined driveway and lagoons and even a golf course. . .no wonder people jumped at the chance to sink their money into it! But we've shilly-shallied for months, and what do we have to show for it? Ninety acres of barren desert." He pointed a finger in Nathan Showalter's direction. "What are you going to do to get this project moving?"

Catherine gasped at the challenge. Nevertheless, she didn't feel overly concerned. Her boss seemed to have an absolute genius for being able to turn the most acrimonious situation into one of camaraderie and good will. She had seen him apply his skill to similar occasions before. If anyone could defuse this tension, he could.

And Nathan Showalter did not disappoint. He rose to stand beside the easel holding a large artist's rendering. His unruffled demeanor exuded a calm that had an immediate soothing effect.

"Let's not let our feelings run too high, gentlemen. While I know all of us hoped to see the project nearer completion by this point, it is hardly a lost cause."

"That's easy for you to say, Showalter." Ellis Todd glared at him across the table. "But I've scheduled meetings with some of our investors from California. They're due here in just a few weeks. They'll expect to see more progress than this when they arrive. How long am I supposed to tell them they have to wait?"

A murmur of agreement rumbled through the assembly.

Catherine waited for his answer with interest. She had written a report on the project herself, describing it in glowing terms gleaned from Mr. Showalter's notes.

"Hardly any time at all." Mr. Showalter turned to the drawing and indicated a large, crescent-shaped area. "We've already begun excavation on the lagoons. Work in that section and on the golf course will begin immediately and should be far enough along to satisfy your investors by the time they arrive. I'm sure they'll understand the slight delay."

"Not if they don't see any progress on the hotel itself," Todd persisted. "The project won't be worth a cent if they expect to find it under construction and the only thing standing on the spot is a rundown shack."

"You can put your worries to rest on that score." Mr. Showalter rested his hands on the table. "I fully recognize that the Phoenician is our most prestigious endeavor. I am not about to let any of us miss this auspicious opportunity. I intend to assume ownership of the property we require within the next couple of weeks."

A bark of laughter cut across the collective sigh of relief. Abner Schwartz stuck out his chin. "If you're expecting the old geezer to turn loose of that land anytime soon, you've got another thing coming."

"What are you talking about, Abner? Explain yourself."

"One of my men talked to him just yesterday. The crazy old coot refuses to sell."

Mr. Showalter's fingers pressed into the surface of the table until their tips turned white. "What do you mean, he refuses?"

"He says he's been on that patch of land for half his life and he doesn't intend to move off just to please some land-hungry latecomers. His term, not mine. This may put a crimp in our plans that even you can't work your magic on, Nathan."

Mr. Showalter rubbed his hands together and smiled. "On the contrary. You know how I love a challenge. I think that's all for today, gentleman. I'll look into the issue Abner brought up and plan to have pleasant news for you at our next meeting."

Taking her cue, Catherine set down her notepad and went to unlock the front door to let them leave. When the last man exited, she locked the door and hurried back down the hallway. The sooner she put everything to rights, the sooner she could get home. She hoped Mrs. Abernathy had remembered to make a cold supper for her.

"That got a little interesting, didn't it?" Mr. Showalter's smile looked genuine, if a bit strained. Little wonder, considering the wringer those people had put him through.

Catherine smiled back and helped him return the easel to its place in the corner, then started putting the room back in order. She swept a stack of papers into a neat pile and riffled through the pages. "I don't see the projected figures for expenses on the work on the golf course. I know it was with these sheets when we started."

Mr. Showalter closed the curtains and reached for his hat. "The golf course expense sheet? I probably slipped it under the corner of the blotter."

Catherine retrieved the paper from under the blotter and waggled it at him with a look of mock sternness. "No wonder you can never find what you need, the way you keep tucking things under there." She slipped the page in place and put the lot back in the filing cabinet.

"That's why I have you here, to keep me in line." He smiled and held her coat for her.

The lines around his eyes looked deeper than usual, she

thought. Today's meeting must have been more difficult for him than he wanted to admit. She slipped her arms into the sleeves and smiled her thanks when he slid the coat up over her shoulders.

Reminded of Mattie's concerns over her spending so much time alone with her boss, she studied his features, only inches away. She had to admit they were handsome enough, even with the lines of strain etched in his face.

A good-looking man and a powerful one—it should be easy enough to feel attracted to him. But being near him didn't produce anything like the electrifying sensation she felt whenever Mitch was around.

Catherine tucked that knowledge away to ponder later. She surveyed the office and gave a satisfied nod. "I think everything is back in order." Her mouth stretched open in a wide yawn, and she clapped her hand across her lips.

"I knew I'd been working you too hard."

Catherine shook her head, mortified. "Not at all. I'm loving every minute of it. I wouldn't change a thing." Another yawn threatened, and she clamped her lips shut.

Mr. Showalter chuckled and hustled her toward the front door. "Go on. Get out of here and do something more enjoyable with what's left of the day. I don't want my secretary looking pale and worn out in the morning."

Catherine laughed and bade him good-bye, then set off toward Mrs. Abernathy's with a light step. She might be tired physically, but her spirit felt energized. Big things required a lot of work, and she was definitely part of something big. She could hardly be called one of the movers or shakers, but at least she could do her own small part. Even being on the fringe of all the action gave her a sense of importance she'd never known before.

Bands of crimson and gold streaked across the darkening

ky. Catherine spread her arms wide as if to embrace the spectacular display. In the distance, a church bell rang out. She could picture Mattie hurrying along to the evening service and settling herself in her usual pew.

Mitch, too, would be on his way to church. Catherine felt a pang of regret at his disappointment when she told him he'd be working. Coupled with the memory of Mattie's own dismay, a twinge of guilt marred her sense of accomplishment, but only for a moment.

Mattie worried too much. They both did. She could always go to church, but an opportunity to be a part of something so grand only came along once in a lifetime.

Her family would understand that. So would Alex. Wouldn't they? Her steps slowed as she imagined their reaction to her putting in nearly a full day's work on the Lord's Day.

No, they wouldn't approve at all. Catherine felt weighted down by the knowledge then shrugged off her feelings of guilt. The Bible itself said there was nothing wrong with pulling your neighbor's ox out of a ditch on the Sabbath. Didn't that prove there were times when tradition had to bow to necessity?

ten

"Are you sure they don't mind me coming?" Catherine took Mitch's hand and stepped down from his roadster.

He continued to hold her hand even after she stood beside him on the curb. "The Johnsons are wonderful people, and you'll love them. I promise."

"But they don't even know me. Why would they want to have a total stranger over for Thanksgiving dinner?" Catherine glanced longingly at the jaunty little car, wishing she could climb back in and let Mitch whisk her away for a drive out into the desert. Riding in the sporty vehicle had been fun, but she would have enjoyed it more if her nerves hadn't been so on edge.

"Relax." Mitch kneaded her fingers with a gentle pressure. "They don't have any family living nearby so they're always looking for a way to fill the empty seats around their table. They've pretty much adopted me since my mother moved back to Indiana."

He cupped her elbow in his hand and led her up the walk to the white stucco house. "As for them not knowing you, I introduced you to them that first Sunday morning at church."

"Did you?" Catherine fiddled with the latch on her purse. "I met so many people that day, I guess I don't remember them all."

Mitch smiled and twisted the door bell. "They remember you."

The look in his eyes sent a warm glow through her. Any remaining feelings of being an outsider were swept away the moment the door opened and she found herself enfolded in a motherly embrace.

"Welcome, my dear! We're so happy you could come."

"Thank you for having me," Catherine said as soon as she could catch her breath.

A joyous smile wreathed her hostess's round face. She turned toward the back of the house and called, "Pete, they're here!"

Mr. Johnson, his lean frame a counterpoint to his wife's plumpness, ambled into the room. He peered at Catherine over the top of his glasses. "We're sure glad you could come. That smile of yours brightens up the whole room."

Before she could respond, Mrs. Johnson put in, "I'm just ready to put things on the table, Catherine. You can help me carry in the food."

Preparations flowed quickly from that point. With no time to feel awkward, Catherine found herself feeling like a member of the household. In what seemed only a few minutes, Mitch was helping her into her chair and seating himself next to her.

After Mr. Johnson said grace, his wife looked over at Mitch. "Have you heard from your mother lately?"

He spread his napkin in his lap and nodded. "I got a letter just yesterday. She's over her bout with the grippe and seems to be feeling better than she has in some time. She'll be spending the day with her brother and his family."

Catherine's mind flew to her own family. What would they be doing today? Her mother, father, and brother would have set off for her grandparents' home early that morning, in plenty of time for the women to put the finishing touches on the holiday meal. More than likely, her grandmother would have invited others to share the dinner with them.

Who would be sitting in Catherine's usual chair? A twinge of homesickness smote her. She ordered herself to focus on the moment instead of looking back. She had a new life now, her own life. Grandma Elizabeth didn't get to go back home for the holidays once she'd made the decision to venture out to Arizona. Surely she must have felt the same loneliness from time to time. But she had gotten through it somehow. Catherine could, too.

Bowls and platters were passed around the table, and the plates were heaped high with Mrs. Johnson's delicious cooking. Catherine feasted on turkey, stuffing, and sweet potatoes until she thought she would explode if she put one more morsel in her mouth.

Mr. Johnson folded his napkin and laid it next to his plate. "And now comes my favorite part of the meal. We're coming up on the start of the Christmas season, when we celebrate the birth of our Savior. Seems to me this is the perfect time to reflect on what He has done for us over the past year. Let's take a few minutes to talk about the things we're grateful for."

His wife patted her lips with her napkin and nodded. "Why don't you start?"

Mr. Johnson cleared his throat. "My heart is overflowing with gratitude for a number of reasons." He sent a warm look toward his wife at the opposite end of the table. "The Lord gave me the finest woman any man could be married to, and He's blessed us with another year together. That's plenty to be thankful for, right there.

"But on top of that, I want to say that I've been in this territory for thirty years now. I've seen it grow and prosper, and it looks like great strides have been made this year in moving toward that day we've all been waiting for. Next year, I hope to be able to say I'm thankful for Arizona being the forty-seventh state in the union."

"Hear, hear," the rest of them chorused.

"I'll go next." Mrs. Johnson folded her hands across her waist. "I'll say the same thing I did last year: When our boy,

Paul, moved away to St. Louis, things got very lonely for Pete and me. I'm thankful the Lord brought Mitch along to help fill the gap.

"And this year I give special thanks for him bringing his young lady to spend the day with us." She smiled sweetly in Catherine's direction. "Why don't you go next, dear?"

It took a moment for Catherine to gather her thoughts. "There are a lot of things for me to be grateful for. The weather, for one thing. That clear blue sky today is a far cry from Thanksgiving with six inches of snow on the ground." Everyone laughed along with her, but then she sobered. "Beyond that, God has blessed me with a wonderful job, a place where I have a chance to make a difference."

She glanced at Mitch. Should she say anything about him, or not? She didn't dare mention the feelings that had been growing in her heart. Still, she couldn't leave him out altogether.

"And He's given me some special friends here," she added. The comment fell far short of what she wanted to say, but it was the best she could come up with on a moment's notice. She flicked a quick look in his direction. Had she said enough? Had she said too much? His expression didn't give her any clue.

"It looks like I'm the one to wind things up," he said. "I have more to be thankful for this year than any other I can remember. My articles are gaining acceptance and building a readership for me, and I have a boss who is willing to let me expand my writing opportunities."

Catherine's heart beat in double time when he cast a sidelong glance her way.

"And I'll echo Catherine's sentiment as well," he added. "I'm thankful for. . .special friends." He reached under the table and clasped her fingers in his.

Catherine felt sure her face was beet red. She picked up her tumbler and took a sip of water to cover her confusion.

Mrs. Johnson reached over and patted her hand. "We've missed seeing you in church, dear. I've hoped you'd be able to accompany Mitch more often. Our pastor has been giving some wonderful messages lately. He feeds our souls as well as we've fed our bodies today. I'm sure you would enjoy them."

The glow Catherine felt after Mitch's secret touch fled. She looked down at the tablecloth, avoiding eye contact. "I'm sure I would," she said and left it at that. She slipped her fingers from Mitch's grasp and busied herself helping Mrs. Johnson clear the table.

The only point of contention in her growing friendship with Mitch had been the times she'd had to turn down his invitations to church. It wasn't her fault, though, that she had to work on Sunday. She knew her sporadic church attendance disturbed Mitch, but it couldn't be helped. She lined up two serving dishes on the kitchen counter and went back to the table for more.

Times were changing, and they all had to accept that fact. They lived in the twentieth century now, and some of the old ways of doing things were bound to pass away.

Still, it just didn't feel right somehow. She set a handful of silverware in the sink and picked up a cloth to wipe down the kitchen counter. Sometimes progress demanded sacrifice. Right now she had to sacrifice her own time for the greater good of the territory.

She had accepted that. She just hoped Mitch could.

❧

The bulb in the green-shaded desk lamp flickered, then came back on full strength. Or maybe it was his eyesight that had flickered. Mitch pinched the bridge of his nose between his thumb and forefinger and glanced at his study window. Pitch black outside. He checked his pocket watch and groaned.

In only a few more hours, the first streaks of dawn would lighten the sky. If he had a lick of sense, he'd get at least a bit of rest before he went in to work at the *Clarion*. He rose and switched off the lamp, more than ready to head for his waiting bed.

Halfway there, he pivoted on his heel. Who was he kidding? If he didn't figure out what had been bothering him for the past few hours, he'd never get a bit of sleep. He returned to the desk and switched the lamp back on again.

"All right, Brewer, focus."

He fastened his bleary gaze on the scraps of papers and pages of notes spread before him and tried to get his mind to cooperate. Somewhere in that untidy heap lay the cause of his late night vigil. But where?

His evening had started out simply enough. The profiles he'd written were proving eminently successful, but they would hold people's interest for only so long. If he wanted to continue to build on his success, Mitch knew he would have to come up with something fresh.

Thanks to Nathan Showalter, he believed he'd found the perfect means of doing just that. During their interview, a chance comment the businessman had dropped in regard to real estate development had planted the tiny seed of an idea that had grown and blossomed as the focus for a whole new set of articles.

The more Mitch dug into the subject, the more excited he became. If he could clearly show the growth potential along with descriptions of the projects various development groups had in mind, the resulting series could not only enhance his career but boost investment in Arizona, as well.

Until tonight, it looked like he was well on his way to doing just that. Until the point when his subconscious realized that, no matter how rosy things looked on the surface, they simply weren't adding up. Like a bad smell floating in the air, he caught the scent of something amiss.

The thought niggled at him all evening and well into the night while he sorted his notes and tried to decide on the best approach for the articles he planned. The more he tried to ignore it, the more it refused to go away.

"Where is it, Lord? It has to be right in front of me, but I just don't see it."

He gathered his papers and shuffled them around. Maybe looking at things from a different perspective would help. He laid the notes out in random order, hoping his subconscious mind would take over and sort things out for him.

His hand paused in the act of laying a sheet of paper on his desk. There it was, right where it had been all the time. Like the last piece of a jigsaw puzzle, the bits of information fell neatly into place.

Mitch stared at the lists in front of him, hoping he could make them mean something other than he feared they did. Try as he might, he couldn't.

He pursed his lips and sucked in a slow breath. If he was right, his research pointed to some serious skullduggery, and from someone highly placed.

His stomach tightened. Assuming he was right, and all this came to light. . .

The implications staggered him. If word of this got out, it could create a scandal that would have far-reaching effect, maybe even have an impact on Arizona's hopes for statehood.

His reporter's instincts kicked into high gear. If wrong was being done, it had to be brought to light. But he couldn't go off half-cocked. He needed the facts—all of them—before he could make an accurate assessment.

Pale threads of light seeped past the curtain. Mitch recognized the herald of a new day but focused on the job at hand.

He could sleep another time.

He pored over his notes, seeing them in a whole new light. Little by little, a pattern emerged. Someone was systematically buying up large tracts of land in the outlying areas.

Nothing wrong with that, in and of itself. With statehood on the near horizon, it was no secret that the value of land around the capital was bound to increase in a big way. All a speculator had to do was buy up all the desert land he could afford and resell it later at a handsome profit. Someone with a fair amount of money to invest could make millions.

Still no surprises there. That was just good business. What intrigued Mitch was the comparison of recent sales and purchase amounts, which led to two very interesting questions: Why, on the brink of a boom in land values, had the current owners decided to sell? And why were they all willing to settle for such low prices?

He had no idea. Yet.

Finding the answers would take time. . .and some delicate investigation. If the wrongdoing ran as deep as he suspected, this wasn't the kind of thing a person could ask about straight out.

Money had immense power to corrupt. With so much at stake, a man's life could become a cheap commodity. Mitch had no intention of treating his own life lightly. Over the years, he'd learned a few tricks of the reporter's trade for finding informants. It was time to put out a few feelers.

A shaft of sunlight darted between the crack in the drapes and caught him full in the eyes. It was also time to get ready for work.

⁂

Mitch got to the Southwestern office that evening just before Catherine and Mattie stepped outside. Catherine's eyes lit up at the sight of him, and Mitch's heart swelled. To see that look, he would have waited outside all afternoon.

He tipped his hat. "May I walk you ladies home?"

"That would be lovely." Catherine's smile was radiant. "We'll be honored to have such a gallant escort, won't we, Mattie?"

Mattie shook her head. "Count me out. I need to stop by Woolworth's on my way home. But the way you two close out the rest of the world when you're together, you'll never miss me." The wink she gave them took any sting out of her words. "See you at dinner."

Mitch held out his arm, and Catherine tucked her hand into the crook of his elbow. They strolled along Jefferson, watching the Christmas shoppers dart in and out of the downtown stores.

"Have you heard anything from Alex or any of your folks back home?"

"My grandmother wrote just the other day." Catherine's face glowed with a tender light. "She's been in the territory for nearly forty-five years, and to hear her talk, you'd think reaching statehood was all her doing! She's determined to come down for the celebration whenever the day arrives. I wish I had a car like yours. I'd love to drive up there and bring her and Grandpa back down with me. It would be something they'd always remember."

Mitch chuckled. "Mine would be too small, I'm afraid. It only holds two people." Inspiration glimmered like one of the electric street lamps that lit their way. "What if I asked my boss if I could borrow his touring car when the time comes? We could go up there together and bring your grandparents back in grand style."

Catherine wrapped both hands around his arm and squeezed. "That would be wonderful! I'll write and let her know. It'll give them something special to look forward to."

Mitch pressed his palm over her hands and smiled down at her. *That was a suggestion worth making.* Now all he had to do was clear it with Dabney.

"How are things going at work?" he asked, more to keep listening to Catherine's voice than from any curiosity about Southwestern's inner workings.

"It's busier than ever. Between keeping up with Mr. Showalter's correspondence and scheduling meeting after meeting, I barely get a chance to catch my breath." She laughed. "But I have to admit I love it. It's going better than I ever expected. What about you?"

"I wish I could say the same thing." Mitch started to continue, but his mouth stretched wide in a yawn.

Catherine turned a teasing look his way. "Not getting enough beauty sleep these days?"

"That's pretty close to the truth. I haven't been sleeping a lot. I've been trying to do some investigating in my off hours, but I'm not getting very far. It seems like everywhere I turn, I run into a dead end."

"I'm sorry." Sympathy colored Catherine's voice. "Would it help to talk about it?"

"Honestly, I'd rather think about something more pleasant. Have you heard any more news from home?"

Catherine laughed. "Probably more than you'll be interested in hearing." She went on to relate details of family life her grandmother had passed along.

Mitch contented himself with listening to her happy chatter, glad he'd been able to steer the conversation away from the subject that had been keeping him awake most nights. Not even to Catherine was he willing to voice his suspicions. If it turned out he was wrong, then he saw no point in casting aspersions on the innocent. If he were right. . .the possible repercussions were more than he wanted to think about.

Right now, it was enough to enjoy the warmth of Catherine's hand through his sleeve and dare to believe that perhaps not every area of his life was headed for a dead end.

eleven

The clear blue skies of early December gave way to a week of dismal gray. The leaden clouds overhead matched the mood of the scene Mitch strode through. He pulled his woolen scarf tighter around his neck. Winter in Phoenix might be a lot warmer than most other parts of the country, but that chilly north wind still carried a bite.

Mitch quickened his pace. It was a good thing he trusted his informant. This wasn't an area of town he would have chosen to visit on his own. The gathering gloom of dusk didn't help his frame of mind a bit. He stepped past a group of seedy-looking men huddled against a brick wall to keep out of the wind.

Following the directions he'd been given, Mitch rounded the next corner. A cluster of broken-down adobe buildings came into view. He paused for a moment to take a closer look. He felt sure his information had been passed along in good faith, but he wasn't about to go waltzing into an isolated place like that without giving it a thorough once-over.

"I don't see anything amiss there, Lord. If You do, I'd sure appreciate it if You'd let me know." He crunched across the gravel and entered the circle of broken buildings.

"Anyone here?" he called in a low voice.

Silence. His whole body tensed as he strained to catch any furtive sounds of approach. . .or flight. Nothing stirred save the wind soughing through the holes in the walls.

I should have known. Mitch jammed his hands in his coat pockets and turned, ready to leave. Then he heard it: faint footsteps scraping across the gravel. He braced himself.

"Are you Brewer?" a voice behind him rasped.

Mitch spun around, ducked into a crouch. He let out his breath and relaxed when he caught sight of his visitor.

The slight man with the wispy gray hair grinned, his lips spreading wide to show a smile that was missing a few teeth. "Don't guess I look any too scary, do I?"

Mitch wanted to laugh out loud. The fellow looked like a stiff breeze would carry him into the next county. He wiped his hand across his mouth to hide his smile. "I'm Brewer. And you're. . ."

"Elmer Watson. I'm the one who sent word and asked to meet with you. I hear you're interested in finding out more about who's buying up all the land around here."

Mitch nodded slowly, not taking his eyes off the man. "I'm also interested in anyone who wants to talk to me about it. I did some checking, and it's a funny thing—I couldn't find a record of Elmer Watson anywhere."

The old man's cackle bounced off the adobe walls. "You're a sharp one, all right." He spat on the ground, then leaned forward confidingly. "Truth to tell, I'm glad you figured that out. If I could have pulled something that easy over on you, so could the other side. Maybe you're worth talking to after all."

Mitch grunted at the backhanded compliment. He decided not to waste time. The desert wind was getting colder by the minute, and this place gave him the willies. "So who are you, really, and what can you tell me about what's going on?"

The old man stared at him for a long moment, then nodded as if he'd made up his mind. "All right, here's the story. My name's Edgar Wheeler, and I own ten acres east of here, over near the Salt River."

Mitch pursed his lips and let out a soft whistle. "Interesting location. I'd say you'll be sitting on a regular gold mine before long. Assuming you're interested in selling, that is."

"Nope." Wheeler's watery blue eyes hardened, taking on a steely look in the gathering dusk. "I came here back in '88 and built me a house out of adobe and river rock. Some sawbones back in St. Joe told me I'd live longer if I moved to a drier climate. Appears he was right—I've lasted a good fifteen years longer than anyone thought I would, me included."

He peered off toward Papago Peak. "I may not have done much with the place, but it's mine, and I plan to stay on it until the day I die. That decision was easy enough to make. Getting those yahoos to listen, that's been the hard part."

Mitch's pulse quickened. "Which yahoos would that be?"

"Those fellows who keep insisting they're going to buy it from me, that's who. They just won't take no for an answer." He hitched his pants up higher on his scrawny waist. "If they had any sense, they'd give up and go away, but I'll outlast 'em, you can count on that."

Mitch smiled down at the feisty codger. "You have clear title to the land?"

"Filed down at the courthouse, all legal and proper. It's mine, no question about that. The only question is whether those coyotes are going to let me live in peace or keep hectoring me."

"What kind of hectoring are you talking about?"

"So far it's just been harsh talk and a couple of broken windows. Nothing I can't handle. But I'm expecting them to up the ante before long, like they did with old Joe Fletcher."

Mitch felt his whole body tense. Maybe he was on the right track at last. "What happened with Fletcher?"

"Those lowlifes came in and offered him a price so low it made him laugh. But then they started coming out to his place every day and trying to get him to sign the sale papers. He kept telling them no—even ran them off with a shotgun once or twice. Then one day he came back from town and found his barn burned to the ground."

Wheeler spat again. "That did it for him. He took the measly price they offered him and lit out of town."

This is it. It has to be. "Where was his property located?"

"It's the place next to mine. Twenty-five acres of desert. Fletcher thought maybe once the dam came in, he could try a little truck farming, but other than that the place isn't anything to make that much fuss over."

Not unless they had reason to expect the value of that property to soar in the near future. Mitch tried to keep the excitement from showing in his voice. "So you're saying he was forced out by these people."

Wheeler scratched his ear. "According to them, he chose to sell of his own free will. That's true enough, I guess, if you mean he chose to take what they paid and leave to get them to quit pesterin' him. Not my idea of having a real choice, though. And as far as I'm concerned, I've already made my decision. I'm going to stay there as long as there's breath in this old body."

"Do you know of any others this has happened to? If I'm going to write about it, I'm going to need as many details as you can give me."

"So you can check them out, same as you did me and that fake name, eh?" The gap-toothed grin split Wheeler's face again. "Get your pencil ready, son. I've got plenty I can tell you."

Voices echoed near the empty buildings. Wheeler swung around, suspicion sharpening his features. "I have to leave. You go ahead and look into what happened to Fletcher. I'll be back in touch as soon as it's safe." With that, he darted through a gaping doorway and disappeared.

Mitch picked his way back to his roadster as quickly as he could, then stood watching before he turned over the engine. Nothing moved. No shadowy figures threatened. Nevertheless,

Wheeler's sense of urgency infected him. He started the car and hurried home, already planning the research he would set in motion.

❧

Catherine smiled when she saw Mitch at the bottom of the steps. Having him wait for her and walk her home could easily become a habit.

"Hi," she said, and matched her steps to his as they strolled toward her boardinghouse. Sometimes Mattie accompanied them; other times she grumbled about being a fifth wheel, but Catherine knew her complaining was all in fun.

Mitch didn't meet her every night. There were the evenings when she had to work late, as well as the times he had to cover a story or go haring off on that mysterious investigation of his. He still didn't talk about that much and changed the subject every time she brought it up. Her curiosity continued unabated, but she determined not to press him. Surely he would tell her about it in his own good time.

Speaking of things she wished he would tell her. . . Catherine slanted a look up at Mitch, her heart quickening at the sight of his lean profile. She grew more certain of her feelings toward him every day. Would he ever let her know whether they were reciprocated?

For the time being, she contented herself with knowing they had become good friends. Well, content might not be quite the right word. Why couldn't a woman take the initiative when it came to declaring her feelings? Waiting for a man to make up his mind to speak seemed to add an unconscionable amount of time to the process.

Catherine thought of herself as a modern woman, but she wasn't about to come right out and tell him how she felt. That would be going too far. Still. . .maybe she could nudge things in the right direction.

"I've been wanting to ask you something," she said before she lost her nerve. "Mr. Showalter is hosting a party on Christmas Eve. It's mostly for his business acquaintances, but he's asked me to come. I wondered if you would be my escort."

As soon as the words were out, she clamped her lips tight and feigned interest in the cracks in the sidewalk.

"Christmas Eve?" Mitch didn't sound put off at all. "That could be fun. I'm sure your boss puts on quite a spread."

"Then you'll do it?" She hoped she didn't sound too eager.

Mitch chuckled. "Did you really think I'd pass up the opportunity to spend time with my favorite girl? Of course I will."

Catherine lost herself in a happy daze then realized he was speaking again. "What did you say?"

"I said it only seems like a fair exchange. I was going to ask you to have Christmas dinner with me. The Johnsons went to St. Louis to spend the holidays with their son. I thought we'd have lunch at the Bellmont; then maybe we could go for a long drive. . .if that's okay with you."

"That would be lovely." *More than lovely, absolutely wonderful!* Catherine congratulated herself for not doing a war whoop right there on the street. Being with Mitch two days in a row and having him all to herself on Christmas Day! It seemed almost too good to be true, and yet there he stood, smiling down at her.

❧

Names and dates. Sales amounts. Property descriptions. Mitch rearranged the slips of paper containing the information he had gleaned, sorting them into new configurations. *It truly is like a puzzle*, he thought. He had nearly all the data he needed. All he had to do was find the right combination, and the pieces would fall into place.

If only Wheeler would make contact again! Now that he

knew a few more of the right questions to ask, Mitch had the feeling one more conversation with the skittish little man would give him what he needed to tie up all the loose ends.

Why hadn't Wheeler sent word? The question had plagued Mitch ever since their interrupted conversation. More than once, he'd cranked up his roadster and headed out toward the old sourdough's property. And every time he'd turned the car around and headed back to town before accomplishing his mission.

He needed to talk to Wheeler, needed to glean the final details that would help him piece everything together and shed light on the shadowy figures behind the goings-on. And hopefully put to rest the uneasy questions that had been growing in Mitch's mind.

But Wheeler's jitters had been no act. Mitch felt sure his informant honestly believed himself to be in danger. If he had gone to all the trouble of setting up a clandestine meeting in a shady part of town, he wouldn't appreciate having Mitch show up on his doorstep. No, he would just have to wait for Wheeler to make contact in his own time, no matter how much the delay frayed his nerves.

That skullduggery was afoot—and on a large scale—he had no doubt. Every scrap of evidence he turned up only served to confirm it. Land was being purchased at rock-bottom prices, on friendly enough terms if the owners went along with the proposed sale, or by whatever means of persuasion necessary if they balked.

Mitch understood the "why" of it. As soon as Taft signed the statehood bill, those tracts of land would multiply at least tenfold in value. For a relatively small investment, its owners stood to make a sizeable fortune. While he decried the motive behind it, it didn't surprise him in the least. Greed had been a common sin as long as man had inhabited the earth.

It was the "who" of the matter that puzzled him. Try as he might, he couldn't pin down the identities of the men responsible for the purchases. Despite his best efforts and repeated trips to the county courthouse, the men remained shadowy, faceless figures who seemed determined to operate unseen, hidden by a paper trail of holding companies and multiple transfers.

His relentless research had brought a few facts to light, though. And despite his intent to search for the truth, Mitch almost wished he hadn't dug so far this time. He pulled his notepad over to him and reviewed the notes he'd taken. The ownership of properties shifted from individuals to land developers to holding companies and back again. And in sorting out the maze of transfers, one name came up again and again: Southwestern Land and Investments.

Did Nathan Showalter have any idea his firm was being used as a front for something so underhanded? Mitch found it hard to believe the man could be totally unaware of any connection with what amounted to land fraud on a grand scale. But given the impression he had formed during their interview, he found it equally difficult to swallow the notion the developer could be guilty of complicity with such a scheme.

He needed to talk to Showalter. The man deserved to know he was being used as a pawn. Mitch pushed back his chair, prepared to crank up his roadster and head straight to Showalter's office.

But what was he supposed to do when Nathan Showalter asked him for proof? This sorry mess had to involve people he knew, people he trusted. He wouldn't accept such wild claims without concrete evidence.

Mitch settled back into his chair reluctantly, ready for action yet unwilling to set in motion events he might regret. He needed the solid proof Wheeler promised to give him, and he needed it now. Where was the man?

What about Catherine? The thought struck him with the force of a blow. Should he mention his suspicions to her? He toyed with the idea, turning it this way and that. Would it be to her benefit to know? *No,* he decided. It would be a mistake. She worked closely with Showalter and sat in on all those after-hours meetings he held. If she suspected one of the men he was involved with and let those suspicions show. . .

If the people behind this had no qualms about strong-arming other men, what would they do to a woman? He couldn't say a word to her until he had every fact in place.

Everything hinged on being able to get that information from Wheeler. Assuming he ever got back in touch.

twelve

"Are you sure you're warm enough?" Mitch furrowed his eyebrows.

"I'll be fine." Catherine settled the lacy shawl around her shoulders and tried not to let him see the laughter that bubbled up inside her, remembering the Christmas Eves of her youth. She wouldn't be surprised if snow already blanketed the ground in Prescott. A Phoenix winter night seemed positively balmy in comparison. And even if the thermometer had registered a temperature worthy of the frozen north, Mitch's look of tender concern would have created warmth aplenty.

She allowed him to escort her to his roadster idling at the edge of the street. He cupped her elbow in his hand and matched his steps to hers. His attentiveness made her feel like a China doll, fragile and precious.

A light breeze touched her cheek, bringing an unexpected shiver. Maybe she was getting acclimated to the warmer climate after all. Or was it from the excitement of spending this special evening in Mitch's company?

They reached the car, and he helped her up onto the running board. His fingers felt warm through the thin fabric of the shawl, and another shiver ran down her arms to her fingertips. Catherine knew then: That chill wasn't due to the temperature at all.

She settled back against the leather seat and watched Mitch round the front of the car and step into the driver's seat. She enjoyed watching him, she admitted to herself. He moved with the easy grace she was used to seeing in the cowboys she'd grown up with.

Mitch released the parking brake and let out the clutch. He was a careful driver, concentrating on guiding the little roadster over the dirt roads rather than making conversation. That suited Catherine just fine. Dusk had settled a thin veil of darkness across the valley. She turned her head slightly so she could watch him without making it obvious.

In the dim light that still remained, she could make out the clean lines of his chin, set at a determined angle while he steered the car along the rutted roads. The sight of his profile and the warmth of his shoulder pressed against hers in the narrow front seat made her heart race right along with the engine. The engine ran more smoothly, though—her heart seemed to be making some strange skips and leaps.

Face it, Catherine. This is one handsome man. The admission didn't help a bit toward calming her racing pulse. Her fingers toyed with the fringe of her shawl, combing through the loose strands of fabric with far greater ease than her mind could sort out her tangled thoughts.

It wasn't only Mitch's good looks that made her attraction to him grow stronger by the day. The more she got to know him, the more she saw his strength of character, his unwavering integrity, the more she felt drawn to him like a nail to a lodestone.

But did Mitch feel the same way about her? She struggled with that question on a daily basis, even while reminding herself of her purpose in coming to Phoenix and the dangers of getting sidetracked from her goal.

With caring came commitment. If she let herself get involved with Mitch, it would take away from the time she could devote to helping the cause of statehood. She might miss out on an opportunity that would never come again. Given all that, did she want him to care?

She wanted him to; there was no getting around that. Not when she caught herself daydreaming about him a dozen times a day. More, if Mattie's count was correct. Catherine's lips twisted in a wry grin.

The road smoothed out, and Mitch took advantage of the respite to turn and meet her gaze. A slow smile lit his face. Catherine's heart picked up its pace even more. The pounding of blood in her temples threatened to drown out the thrum of the engine altogether.

What's the matter with me? In spite of her runaway pulse, she had to laugh at herself.

Growing up in the rough country of Lonesome Valley, she'd faced more than one dangerous situation in her lifetime. She could hold her own with a cantankerous horse. She'd once faced down an ornery bull. While she was just a little girl, she helped track down a band of rustlers. And through it all, her spirit never wavered.

Now one man's nearness was enough to reduce her to a quivering jelly.

The road reclaimed Mitch's attention, and Catherine let her restless thoughts resume their dance through her mind. What did Mitch feel for her? The question grew more important to her with each passing moment.

His face lit up every time she came in sight. Then again, he smiled at Mattie, too. Mitch had shown himself unfailingly polite in all his dealings with women. Could the pleasure he showed in her presence simply be a matter of courtesy? The thought rattled her more than the roadster's jouncing.

But what about tonight? Would he have accepted her invitation with such alacrity if he didn't feel something more than mere friendship for her? She discounted the notion that he merely needed a pleasant way to spend his Christmas Eve. Mitch was both good-looking and popular. She had seen the way both men and women responded to him. No, it couldn't be a matter of him not having other possibilities for the evening's entertainment. That was one mark on the plus side of the ledger.

Then there was that moment at the Johnsons' Thanksgiving dinner, the time when he spoke of being thankful for special friends. That hadn't been her imagination. Neither had the pressure of his fingers on hers beneath the shelter of the table.

The car jolted in and out of a pothole that must have been large enough to hide a jackrabbit. Catherine grabbed at the side of the seat to keep from banging her head on the roof.

"Sorry. I didn't see that one coming." Mitch's jaw tightened as he wrestled the car back under control.

"It's all right." More than all right. What were a few potential bumps and bruises when everything in her mental tally added up to Mitch having feelings for her?

Before her jangled thoughts could settle back down, they reached their destination. Bright lights shone from every window in the large house and spilled outside.

Vehicles lined both sides of the street. Mitch parked the roadster behind a Daimler touring car and gave a low whistle. "Looks like your boss runs with some pretty high rollers."

"Some of the most important people in the territory will be here tonight." Catherine could hear the pride in her voice. She waited while Mitch set the parking brake and hurried around to her side of the car to help her alight. When he touched her arm this time, the chill was replaced by a ripple of electricity that reminded her of the tingle in the air that presaged a thunderstorm.

But the sky was clear tonight. The only danger of a storm lay in her wayward, tumultuous heart.

"It looks like things are already under way." Catherine took Mitch's arm and let him help her across the uneven ground.

When he placed his hand on the small of her back to guide her around a small bush, she caught her breath in a quick gasp, then tried to collect herself. She couldn't go in there behaving like a smitten schoolgirl! Somehow she had to get her emotions under control.

She risked a glance up at Mitch and saw something in his eyes that made her heart threaten to pound right out of her chest. Their steps slowed as if by mutual consent, and they stood just outside the pool of light, staring into each other's eyes.

Mitch reached out and traced the line of her jaw with his forefinger. Catherine's eyelids fluttered closed. Even without the benefit of sight, she sensed him drawing nearer. Her lips trembled, and she had to concentrate in order to breathe.

Raucous laughter burst out behind them. Two couples stepped out of a touring car and made their way up the front walk.

The fragile moment shattered like splintered glass.

Mitch drew back. "I guess we'd better go in."

Catherine could only manage a nod in response.

He led her to the front door, and they stepped into a party already in full swing. Festive decorations hung from every available surface, and a din of chatter filled their ears. Catherine felt her spirits rise as she viewed the swirl of activity, delighted to see a number of prominent personages among the guests.

Two months ago, they would have been nothing more than names mentioned during a discussion of territorial events or read about in newspaper articles. Now she recognized the faces that went with those names, both from living in the capital and from meeting a good many of them at Nathan Showalter's evening and weekend meetings.

Some of them recognized her, too. One of the territorial legislators looked her way and smiled in acknowledgment. Catherine nodded in reply, trying to mask the thrill of excitement she felt. That would never have happened if she'd stayed in

Prescott. In only two months she had gone from a little nobody tucked away out on the T Bar to a person known by some of the most important people in the territory. She glanced up to see if Mitch had noticed.

He hadn't. He stood halfway turned away from her, looking in the opposite direction. A pang of disappointment shot through her to be replaced by pleasure when she realized their host was approaching.

"Brewer! Good to see you." Nathan Showalter slapped Mitch on the shoulder before turning to Catherine. His eyes lit in a gleam of approval, and she blessed Mattie for helping her pick out her new aqua dress during their last foray to Goldwaters'. The gown's sleek lines made her look more like someone used to this type of gathering than a mere office worker.

"And Catherine! How lovely you look. I'm sure your escort, here, would agree. It looks like that interview netted you more than just an article, eh?" He nudged Mitch with his elbow.

Mitch frowned and made an abbreviated gesture, as though he wanted to say something, then changed his mind. The front door opened again, and a stream of people flowed into the room.

Mr. Showalter turned to greet the newest arrivals, and Catherine let Mitch guide her toward the refreshment area, festooned with holiday bows and imported German glass decorations.

Eyeing the other women in the room, she took note of their dresses and compared them to her own. A sense of delight took hold of her at the knowledge that her gown was the equal of any of them. The aqua fabric could have been created especially to set off her coloring to best advantage. The gored skirt, gathered in the back, swayed gracefully with every step she took, and the bodice's ivory dot lace inset and the teardrop lace trim around the cuffs and neckline provided the perfect finishing touches.

No longer the frumpy little country girl, she could hold her own in this elegant crowd. The realization was sweet.

Catherine moved along in a happy daze, hearing snatches of bright conversation but not really taking any of it in. She felt the warm pressure of Mitch's hand on her arm, her anchor to keep her from floating right up to the ceiling. Here she was spending Christmas Eve in the company of all the right people with the most handsome man in Phoenix as her escort. Could anything make her life more ideal?

Her mind flitted back to their unfinished conversation on the front lawn. Had Mitch been about to kiss her? Every instinct confirmed it, but she couldn't know for sure. And it was hardly the kind of thing she could ask him.

If he had, what would she be feeling at this moment? Would her life change for the better, or would a romantic entanglement bring chaos in its wake? She had no way of knowing.

"Shall I get us some punch?" Mitch's voice jolted her back to the moment.

"Yes, please." His expression gave her no clue as to whether he regretted the earlier interruption as much as she did. She watched him walk to the punch bowl, then turned her attention to the heavily laden table in front of her. Maybe the lavish assortment of delicacies would help take her mind off a string of what-ifs for which she had no answers.

Mr. Showalter had spared no expense in providing a sumptuous repast for his guests. Dates and spiced pecans tempted her sweet tooth. Farther along the table she saw platters of sliced ham and pheasant, plus an array of foods she couldn't name.

Intrigued by a bite-sized tart, Catherine picked it up and

popped it into her mouth. One bite set her taste buds tingling. She closed her eyes and savored the wonderful fruity taste.

Moving down the table, she sampled a slice of hothouse melon. If her family could see her now! Wouldn't they be amazed at the way their little girl had adapted to life among the elite? Her appetite whetted, she picked up a plate and angled toward the sliced pheasant.

"Here you go." Mitch stood at her elbow, a cup of punch in each hand. He held one out to her, and her fingertips touched his when she accepted it.

Once again she sensed that some powerful force was about to be unleashed. She heard the plate clink against one of the platters when she set it back on the table, her interest in food suddenly vanished.

The cup trembled when she lifted it to her lips. Steeling herself, she raised her gaze to look across the rim into Mitch's eyes and felt like she was plummeting off a precipice with no one to catch her.

She waited for Mitch to speak, but he didn't say a word, just stared back as if he could read the very thoughts of her soul.

Despite the punch, her throat felt as dry as the desert sand. What thoughts lay behind those gray eyes? Could she be wrong in believing she saw her own longing reflected there?

The continued silence unnerved her. She willed him to speak, to say anything. Instead, he took the cup from her nerveless fingers and set it on the table next to his.

"Come on," he said. "Somewhere in all this frivolity, there must be a place where we can talk."

A sense of panic caught Catherine in its coils. "Have you noticed the beautiful decorations?" she heard herself say. "Those glass balls were made in Germany. Mr. Showalter ordered them from San Francisco, just for the occasion."

Enough! she scolded herself, even as she heard herself

spouting still more meaningless chatter. "Such a lot of guests! And so many of them are very influential people."

Mitch didn't seem to mind. For that matter, he didn't seem to hear her. He threaded his way through the press of people with Catherine in tow.

At the doorway to the front parlor, he hesitated. "It's too crowded in here. Maybe we can get outside." He started toward the exit then pointed to his left. "There's an alcove over there. Let's see if we can get to it."

Catherine looked in the direction he pointed and saw a secluded nook just beyond an archway. An archway from which dangled a sprig of mistletoe.

Mitch spotted the mistletoe at the same moment she did. A satisfied grin slid across his face. "The alcove. Definitely the alcove."

Did this mean. . . ? Was he going to. . . ? Catherine's nervousness doubled, and she heard another spate of words burst from her lips. "It looks like this is going to be a special Christmas for us."

Mitch laughed and glanced at her with a question in his eyes.

Catherine sucked in a quick breath and felt her face flame. "For all of us, I mean. For Arizona. Mr. Showalter says this will be our last territorial Christmas. Next year we'll celebrate the holidays as the forty-seventh state."

Mitch, who had been making steady progress toward his goal, froze. His features grew stiff, and his eyes clouded.

"What is it?"

He seemed to pull himself back from a distance. "Nothing." He looked around as if assessing the routes available. "Let's see if we can get past this group." He maneuvered his way between a stocky gentleman and the wall and motioned for Catherine to follow suit.

The alcove lay just ahead. Screened by a large potted palm, it provided a measure of privacy.

Once on the other side of the knot of guests, Mitch drew a deep breath and relaxed. "That's better." He captured both of Catherine's hands and laced his fingers through hers. A tentative smile curved his lips.

But something had happened back there, something that set Mitch on edge. "What is it?" she repeated. "What's wrong?"

Mitch just shook his head. "It isn't important." His thumbs made slow circles on the backs of her fingers, and Catherine felt every nerve ending in her body come alive. He was going to kiss her. Every instinct she possessed told her so.

Much as she wanted that to happen, she couldn't surrender to the delight of being drawn into Mitch's arms until she knew what was going on. She slowed her breathing in an effort to likewise slow the beating of her heart, hoping that would help her think more clearly.

Maybe she was making a mountain out of a molehill. Hadn't her family always teased her about her stubborn nature? She just needed to quit thinking so much and let this magic moment play out of its own accord. She closed her eyes and tried to recapture the electricity she felt earlier.

It was no good. She couldn't give in to her desire until she knew what put that fleeting glint of steel in Mitch's eyes.

With a burst of laughter, the knot of people on the other side of the palms broke up and filtered back to rejoin the main group of guests. Silence settled over the alcove like a fleecy blanket. Mitch stepped back and tugged Catherine along with him. He glanced up to check his location then took one more step backward, positioning himself directly under the mistletoe.

He pulled Catherine closer still. "Does this suggest anything to you?"

Catherine gave her head a tiny shake. "It can't until I find out what's bothering you."

"Right at this moment, not a single thing." His eyes darkened, and his hands slid up her arms to her shoulders. Closing the tiny gap that remained between them, he bent his head and leaned toward her.

Catherine pressed her palms against his chest. "No, something is wrong, and I need to know what it is."

Mitch resisted for a moment then settled back on his heels. He looked down at the floor for a moment then heaved a deep breath. "All right." He gathered her hands loosely in his and fixed her with an unwavering stare.

"You know I've been doing some investigating." He made it a statement instead of a question. "And I may have told you I came across a few things that puzzled me."

Catherine nodded slowly, wondering what this had to do with the two of them and mistletoe.

"One of those things concerns your boss."

Catherine drew her eyebrows together, trying to keep up with this unexpected turn in the conversation. "What about him?"

Mitch stroked the backs of her hands with his thumbs again in a slow, comforting movement. "Something isn't right. There's a big scheme under way that has to do with some of the recent land deals. I've done a lot of digging, trying to get to the bottom of it. I can't prove it. . .yet. . .but everything I've turned up points to Showalter having some involvement in all this."

Catherine's insides felt like they'd congealed. She tried to make sense out of his statement. " 'All this'? You mean the scheme—whatever it is that's wrong?"

Mitch nodded, misery written across his features. "That doesn't mean he's a willing participant," he hastened to add. "There's always the possibility he's just being used. I don't know by whom yet, but he's definitely a part of it."

Catherine snatched her hands free as if yanking them away from an open flame. "Is that why you agreed to come? Was it just some reporter's trick so you could get inside his home and snoop around?"

Mitch opened his mouth, but she cut him off before he could speak. "Don't bother to deny it. It must have seemed like a heaven-sent opportunity." She clenched her hands. "How can you possibly suspect Mr. Showalter of anything like that?"

Mitch's face sagged, and he let his hands drop limply to his sides. "It isn't that I suspect him, exactly. I just know there's something that doesn't look right."

"Doesn't look right? And that's reason enough for you to presume his guilt? I work with the man, remember? I see him every day, and I'm telling you, you're wrong." She stepped back, putting some distance between them. "You found some information that didn't make sense to you, so you've decided some sort of conspiracy exists. But you can't back up that assumption, can you? You haven't been able to find one thing to prove this wild theory of yours."

She whirled and paced the narrow width of the alcove. Her heel struck one of the potted palms and nearly sent it over. "You know what the real problem is, Mitchell Brewer? You're so bent on making a name for yourself, you're seeing evil where none exists." She saw the lines of pain etched across his face but was too angry to care.

"Believe me, Catherine, I'm not taking any of this lightly. Do you think it was easy for me to tell you that?"

"I think you're more interested in headlines than in protecting a respectable man's good name."

"I appreciate your loyalty to him, and I don't want to hurt either one of you. I wouldn't have said a word about it if you hadn't pressed me to."

But if she hadn't forced the issue, she would have thrown open the door of her heart without realizing what he might do for ambition's sake. Tears burned her eyes and clogged her throat. She turned her back on Mitch and spoke in an icy tone. "Take me home."

thirteen

Merry Christmas!

Catherine penned the bright greeting, then stared dully at the sheet of stationery, her mind as blank as the rest of the page. She shifted in the hard-backed chair and looked out her window, hoping the view outside would provide inspiration.

The sun shone in a sky of brilliant blue. Her lips twisted. If there were any justice, the heavens ought to be hung with leaden clouds dropping sheets of rain to echo the despair in her heart. She drew a shaky sigh and turned back to the letter to her family:

I can picture you all sitting around the living room today. Dad has stoked the fireplace to take the chill off the air before he sits down to read the Christmas story. Afterward, you'll be laughing and teasing as you exchange your gifts.

Just as they had every Christmas morning of her life. Her eyes misted, and she paused to swipe at them with her handkerchief.

I, on the other hand, stepped outdoors this morning and barely felt the need for a wrap. This desert air is so clear that I can almost pick out the individual rocks on the side of Camelback Mountain. You'd enjoy it down here, I know, although I confess the mild temperatures hardly make it seem like Christmas.

Neither did the pain that lingered in her heart ever since Mitch had dropped her off the night before. Neither of them had spoken on the drive home, and he hadn't said more than a brief good-bye when he escorted her up to her door. Truth to tell, she hadn't given him an opportunity to do more. Given the coldness of her attitude toward him, it was a wonder frost hadn't formed right there on the doorstep.

She had done the right thing, though, in cutting the evening short. Mitch's suspicion of Mr. Showalter still stung. So did the knowledge that accepting her invitation might have owed as much to wanting to snoop around the Showalter home as to any desire to spend time with her.

At least she hadn't let him kiss her. She still had her self-respect intact. Catherine dipped her pen nib in the inkwell and continued resolutely:

> *I miss you all more than I can say. Still, I can't tell you how much it means to me to be here, especially at this moment in Arizona's history. Great things are about to happen, and I'll be on hand to see them all! And to tell you about it, of course. You'll have your very own firsthand account of all the goings-on, straight from my pen.*

Catherine went over what she had written, looking for anything that would strike a sour note, anything to give the slightest hint to her family that all was not perfectly well in her universe.

In the distance, church bells chimed. Catherine read the cheery missive a second time and lifted her pen again, ready to add a few last lines before her signature.

A series of quick taps rattled the door. Mattie pushed it open and poked her head inside. "Are you busy?"

Catherine summoned up her brightest smile. "Not at all.

I was just writing a Christmas letter to my family. I'm nearly finished."

Mattie slipped inside the room and produced a small, wrapped package from her pocket. "Here. I wanted to give this to you before I leave for church. It isn't much, but I hope you like it."

Catherine took the little parcel and reached in her desk drawer for Mattie's present.

"You go first," Mattie commanded. "I can't wait to see your reaction."

"Oh, Mattie, they're lovely." Catherine looked at the soft linen handkerchiefs in her lap and traced the delicate lace edging with her fingertip.

"I saw you looking at them the last time we went to Goldwaters'," Mattie said with a grin. "I was glad when you didn't buy them so I could give you something I knew you'd like."

"And I do." Catherine laid the snowy squares on the far corner of her desk, safe from contact with the inkwell. Her spirits lifted for the first time since the disaster of the night before. It was Christmas, after all. "Now open yours."

Mattie didn't need a second invitation. She carefully unwrapped the paper Catherine had decorated with sketches of flowers and bows, and crowed with delight when she spied the tiny bottle of perfume and the packet of sugared almonds within. "This is perfect. You know me well."

Catherine had to laugh. "I know your sweet tooth, you mean. Those almonds won't last long, but I hope you enjoy them while they do."

Mattie drew herself up with an affronted air. "Are you implying I won't be able to resist? I'll have you know I have tons of self-restraint." She popped one almond into her mouth, then another. "When I want to, that is."

They both dissolved into giggles, and Catherine wrapped

her arms around the other girl. "Thanks, Mattie. You're a dear friend."

"As are you." Mattie returned the hug. The church bells tolled a second time, and she straightened, glancing at Catherine's small clock. "I need to be going. Are you sure you don't want to come with me?"

Catherine started to answer, but Mattie cut in. "You don't need to make excuses. If I had a chance to spend Christmas Day with someone as nice as Mitch Brewer, I'd jump at it. Have a wonderful time!" She laughed and waved as she went out, leaving Catherine alone with her thoughts.

She managed to keep the smile on her face until the door closed, then sagged back into her chair. All the Christmas cheer seemed to leave when Mattie did, and Catherine's brighter mood with it.

She couldn't blame Mattie for not realizing how her parting comment stung. She remembered their excitement over shopping for the aqua dress.

"You're away from your family," Mattie reasoned, with an air of one who knew about such things. "He's away from his. You're going to spend Christmas Eve and Christmas Day together. Sounds like the man is getting serious." She let out a wistful sigh. "This is so romantic!"

Laughing, Catherine had agreed. It had made perfect sense at the time. She didn't see any need to spoil Mattie's day by telling her things had changed. Neither could she fault Mattie for the emptiness she felt.

You've only yourself to blame for that. And why should you be feeling so miserable? she scolded herself. *You're right where you wanted to be, holding the kind of job you dreamed of.*

All true enough. So why did she feel like a cavern of loneliness had opened up inside her?

She heard the church bells again. She pictured Mattie sliding into her pew. Would Mitch be sitting in his own church, ready to spend the holiday with some of his single friends?

It seemed everyone had a place to belong and someone to belong to today. . .except her. She picked up her pen and held it over the sheet of paper a moment, then scribbled rapidly: *I'll close this wishing you the merriest of Christmases with all my love.*

She signed her name and dashed away her tears before they could trail down her face and splash onto the stationery.

⅔

An eternity passed, although the calendar on her wall assured Catherine it had only been a matter of days since her disastrous date with Mitch. Seven to be exact. Undoubtedly the longest week of her life.

She lifted the current page on the calendar. Tomorrow would usher in the first day of 1912. But where the prospect of a new year once held nothing but bright promise, the idea of going though another twelve months seemed more like a prison sentence.

She let the sheet fall back into place. Tomorrow she could tear it off, assuming she could summon up the energy. Or maybe she would just let it hang there as a reminder of the month her life had gone from joy to despair.

Sensing that something was amiss, Mattie fluttered around like a butterfly. Catherine deflected her questions at first, then came right out and told her to mind her own business, too sick at heart to be able to bring herself to tell her friend how foolish she had been.

She managed to drag herself out of bed every morning, to make herself presentable, and to show up at the office on time. There, she could throw herself into a frenzy of activity, matching pace with Mr. Showalter, who was certain each day brought them that much closer to statehood.

Catherine clutched at those hours at work like a lifeline. Keeping up with the frenetic pace set by her employer was more than a matter of earning her pay. It gave her a reason to get up every morning, to breathe in and breathe out, and otherwise go about the business of living. Once work hours had ended, she returned to the boardinghouse. Ignoring Mrs. Abernathy's tempting dinners, she would flop onto her bed and stare at her ceiling until she fell into a troubled sleep. And then she got up the next day and did it all over again.

Mattie watched from a distance, knowing her concern would not be welcome, but too loyal to abandon her completely.

Maybe the long anticipated Admission Day would spark her back to life. Catherine stretched across her comforter and tried to recapture her former pleasure at the thought of attaining statehood at last. It was no use. Try as she might, she couldn't get past the ache inside. The tears that had scalded her cheeks the first few evenings had dried up under the heat of the anger she now felt. She rolled over onto her side and wrapped her arms around her knees.

Just who was she angry with? Mitch, for daring to question her employer's integrity? Or herself, for the way she lost her temper and treated Mitch so spitefully? If she could answer that question, maybe she could pull herself out of this funk and get back to living again.

A quick knock sounded on her door. *Mattie. Probably with some cheery idea about helping her see in the new year.* Catherine clamped her lips together and refused to answer. If she didn't hear anything, she might just assume Catherine was asleep and go away.

The tapping came again. Catherine stifled a groan and pulled her pillow over her head. She didn't want to see Mattie or anyone else right now.

When the knob rattled and the door swung open, she sat

up, ready to give Mattie a piece of her mind for bursting in uninvited.

Mrs. Abernathy's round face beamed at her. "I'm sorry if I disturbed you, dear, but there's a gentleman downstairs asking for you. I know you've been feeling under the weather lately, but I didn't think you'd want me to send him away."

Catherine pushed herself up off the mattress. "Who is it?"

"He didn't give his name." The landlady's eyes twinkled as she backed out into the hall. "But he certainly is good-looking."

Nathan Showalter would fit that description, Catherine thought. But he would have sent a messenger if he wanted to see her. A man of his stature would hardly go to his secretary's boardinghouse to ask her to come in to the office.

Who else could it be? Her heart sang out a hopeful answer, even as her head squelched the idea. Mitch had no reason to come. Not after the way she had treated him. Her head understood that all too well, but her racing heart refused to listen to reason.

Telling herself she was a fool for daring to hope, Catherine checked her appearance in the mirror and gasped. Her hair dangled about her face in untidy strands. She yanked her brush through the tangles and dressed it in a simple style. There wasn't much she could do about the circles under her eyes. That pallor, though. . .

She pinched her cheeks and bit her lips to bring back some color. She surveyed the results. Hardly a prize-winning effort, but the best she could do under the circumstances. Racing to the head of the stairs, she breathed a prayer that her heart, instead of her head, would be proven right and descended the steps.

Mitch stepped out of shadows near the doorway when she was still four steps from the bottom. Catherine gripped the banister, resisting the impulse to clear the remaining steps with a single leap and hurl herself into his arms.

She tried to arrange her features in an expression of polite inquiry but couldn't keep a joyful smile from spreading across her face.

Mitch turned his hat over in his hands. "I thought you might like to go for a drive."

Catherine completed her descent and tried to collect her whirling thoughts. So much to say, so much to explain. Where should she begin? In the end, she simply looked up at Mitch and nodded. "I'd like that."

&

The roadster bounded its way over bumps and ruts as Mitch guided the jaunty little car along a route that took them north of town. His attention was once again focused on keeping the car on the road, so Catherine contented herself with holding on for dear life and watching the landscape fly by.

As they left the city and its buildings behind, the scenery gave way to a sweeping expanse of desert. The tawny grasses reminded her of home, and she followed the sweep of their lines to the tall mountains that ringed the Valley of the Sun.

These wore a scattering of green on their dusty brown slopes, but a multitude of rock outcroppings eliminated any hint of softness. Nearer to the road where they jounced along, palo verde trees and stately saguaros dotted the landscape, and the scent of greasewood hung in the air.

A harsh land, some would call it, but it was her land, her family's home for three generations.

The road ran right up to the foothills of Camelback Mountain. Mitch followed the track partway up the slope then swung the roadster in a wide loop so they sat facing the western sky, where the sun hung suspended over the horizon like an orange globe. He set the parking brake and turned off the motor. The sudden stillness came almost as a shock after the loud rattling of the engine.

Mitch swiveled so he sat half facing her. "I'll bet you never spent a New Year's Eve halfway up the side of a mountain before."

"Why, I believe you're right." Catherine was grateful for his teasing tone and answered in kind. "Speaking of New Year's Eve, I suppose you've already made a list of resolutions?"

"Only one."

She waited a long moment. "Are you going to tell me what it is?"

"Later." He leaned back against the leather seat and stretched his legs as far as he was able within the confines of the car. The sun edged its way down past the tops of the White Tank Mountains to the west.

A tenuous silence hung between them. Catherine didn't know what to make of the situation. To all appearances, they seemed to be back on their old, easygoing footing, but neither of them had brought up the altercation at the Christmas party. Until they did, could she take anything for granted?

Streaks of copper, peach, and crimson shot out from the dying sun, lengthening the shadows across the land. The mountains in the distance took on a purple hue. Catherine twisted her fingers together. Mitch seemed content just to sit and watch the show of colors, but she couldn't relax until she had made her peace with him.

"There's something I want to say." She knotted her hands in her lap. "I want to apologize for the way I acted last week. I was upset, but I didn't have any right to behave that way. I was cold and unkind to you, and I'm truly sorry." *And I wish I hadn't spoiled that kiss,* she added to herself.

Mitch watched the shadows deepen. The hint of a smile played over his lips.

Catherine bristled. "Are you laughing at me?"

"Not at all. I was planning to apologize myself. I was just thinking that clearing the air this way makes it easier for me to tell you what I have to say."

Uncertain of where this was leading, she tried to match his bantering tone. "Something about your fascination with sunsets?"

"No, about the resolution I made." The teasing note remained in his voice, but it didn't match the intensity in his eyes.

Catherine's heart skipped. "And what might that be?"

Mitch twisted so he faced her fully. The movement brought his knee up next to hers. Catherine pressed her hands against her skirt to blot the dampness from her palms.

Mitch leaned so close she could feel his breath brush her cheek. He focused his gray eyes on hers and held her captive with his gaze. "Never again to let myself get distracted when I'm about to kiss a lovely lady. *This* lovely lady." He slid his arm along the seat behind her, leaned closer, and covered her mouth with his.

Catherine felt his arm tighten, pressing her close against him. Her hands slid up to encircle his neck. Whatever she had dreamed this kiss might hold, reality far surpassed her imagination.

Once again she had that sensation of tumbling off a precipice—falling, falling, with no one to catch her, knowing she had to hit bottom at some point but with no idea whether something would break her fall gently or she'd shatter into a million pieces.

Their lips parted, and Mitch stared at her in the waning light, looking as stunned as she felt. A slow smile curved his lips, and he brought his hand up to cup her cheek. Catherine rested her head against his palm, wishing she could make this moment last forever.

Without saying a word, he tilted his head, and Catherine knew he was going to kiss her again.

"Happy New Year," he murmured, just before his lips touched hers.

fourteen

"Did you hear the news?" Enid asked the moment Catherine set foot inside Southwestern Land and Investments.

"Who could help but hear it?" Catherine marched down the hall to her office, where she took off her hat and stowed her purse in her desk drawer. Mrs. Abernathy had run in from the kitchen during breakfast, waving a copy of the *Phoenix Clarion*.

"Will you look at this?" She held the paper aloft so her boarders could read the headline: NEW MEXICO JOINS THE UNION.

The leaden feeling in Catherine's stomach owed nothing to Mrs. Abernathy's featherlight biscuits and everything to the knowledge that once again Arizona's hopes had been dashed.

If their landlady's announcement hadn't been sufficient, Catherine and Mattie would have found out quickly enough during the few blocks' walk to work. The streets were full of people, all talking in urgent tones, and all saying the same thing: New Mexico had beaten them in the race to win the coveted forty-seventh star on the American flag.

"But what does it mean for us?" Enid persisted.

"For us?" Catherine swung around and faced her coworker. "It means Arizona's entry into the union has been delayed once again. But only that: delayed. We've weathered obstacles on the road to statehood before, but we kept pressing on toward the goal. We'll do the same this time; never fear. The people of Arizona have their goal in sight, and they won't be stopped."

The sting of tears in her throat warned her she'd better

quit talking. She turned back to her desk and pulled out the prospectus she needed to finish, hoping she could follow her own advice. She wasn't afraid, she reasoned, while she lined up her pens along the desktop. Not really. More frustrated than anything.

Yes, frustrated was just the word. That described her feelings and those she'd heard expressed on her way to work that morning. The news of New Mexico's success had everyone's tongue wagging. While Arizonans recognized this as a major event and a sense of uneasy excitement pervaded the air, it was somewhat akin to being the bridesmaid at a sister's nuptials instead of the one wearing the wedding gown.

That sense of frustration spilled over into office life, where the resulting tension became a palpable thing. Enid and Irene bent over their machines, typing diligently and trying not to attract their supervisor's attention.

Mattie, though, failed to find a file quickly enough to satisfy Miss Trautman, who took her to task right in front of the other employees. Hearing the uproar, Mr. Showalter came out of his office and snapped at Miss Trautman. The supervisor made no response, but the angry glint in her eyes promised a tongue-lashing for the office workers as soon as their employer was out of earshot.

After finding herself on the receiving end of still more of her boss's surly behavior, Catherine was perilously close to tears. Seeing her distress, Mr. Showalter reined his temper in with a noticeable effort and apologized. "I'm sorry I've been churlish. I'll try to be more civil."

Catherine dabbed at her eyes surreptitiously and concentrated on her work, not wanting to add to the stress that flooded the office throughout the entire day. She couldn't hold his irritability against him. While all Arizonans shared the disappointment of coming in second to New Mexico, Mr.

Showalter's expectations had been even higher than most. After all his effort, all his hard work, it was no wonder he felt the frustration so keenly.

She put her files back in order, stacked the folders into a neat pile, and straightened the rest of her desk. Tomorrow would be better. Surely he would brighten up again with the passing of time, once he had a chance to get over the initial shock.

Having canceled the meeting planned for that evening at Mr. Showalter's orders, she gathered up her purse and left the office only minutes after the other girls said their good-byes. When she spied Mitch leaning against the front of building, she felt the day's burdens lift off her shoulders.

He smiled in response to her glad hello, and they strolled down Jefferson Street in the direction of her boardinghouse. Catherine enjoyed the companionable silence they shared as they walked along. With Mitch, she never had to worry about keeping up a conversation just to fill the air with words. She could relax with him, simply taking pleasure in his company.

What a difference she felt since making up with him on New Year's Eve! Despite her gloomy expectations, 1912 had started out with a dazzling sense of hope after all. Pleasant thoughts filled her mind. Two blocks later, she glanced up at the object of her daydreams, startled to see a deep furrow between his brows.

"What is it?"

"Nothing."

Catherine felt the corners of her lips tilt upward. "The last time you told me that, things didn't go so well, remember?"

Mitch responded with a faint smile. "I had some news today that rattled me."

"Your mother isn't ill again, is she?"

"No, nothing like that." He walked a few more steps in

silence then added, "Do you remember me talking about that man I was waiting to hear from? His name was Edgar Wheeler. He promised to provide me with the information I needed to figure out who's at the bottom of this land grab."

His face took on a stern, cold look, and Catherine felt a sudden spurt of fear. "Has he changed his mind, decided not to give you the information after all?"

"He can't give it to me. I just got word today that he's dead."

"Oh, Mitch! I'm so sorry."

"That would be bad enough in itself. But it's even worse: He was murdered."

Catherine caught her breath. "Surely not! Are you certain?"

"His body was found out on the edge of the desert. He'd been beaten to a pulp." Mitch's lips drew together in a thin line. "I'm sorry. I shouldn't be telling you all this."

"No, that's all right. If it concerns you, it concerns me."

"I can't help but think part of this is due to my meddling."

"You can't blame yourself. You aren't responsible for his death."

"I'm not so sure. If I'd done something sooner, taken my concerns to the police, maybe he'd be alive today." He pounded his fist against his palm. "He told me he was in danger, and I believed him. . .to a point. I just never believed they would go this far."

"Who?" Catherine said. "You don't still think—"

"At this point, I don't know what to believe. All I know is that Edgar Wheeler died despite my efforts to put a stop to this thing. . .or maybe because of them."

❧

Mitch cranked up his roadster and headed out toward Edgar Wheeler's property. Now that the old man was dead, it couldn't do any harm. He clenched his teeth. Could he have prevented Wheeler's death if he'd followed through on the impulse to visit him earlier? Or would that merely have hastened matters? The questions haunted his every waking hour, but he would never know the answers now.

Following the directions he'd gotten from the clerk at the county recorder's office, he drove east, leaving the city behind him. The road dwindled to a narrow track that led up to the top of a hill. Mitch stopped the car when the path petered out and looked around, frowning.

This had to be the right place. He'd followed the directions exactly. But instead of Wheeler's house, only a pile of rocks adorned the hilltop.

He got out of the roadster and poked through the rubble. Tin cans, a tattered almanac, the remnants of a lonely life. He pulled a crumpled envelope from beneath a chunk of rock and looked at the address: *E. Wheeler*. He had the right place, no doubt about it.

Someone didn't waste any time tearing it down. Mitch looked away from the pile of debris and gazed out across the landscape, entranced by the view this spot commanded. From this vantage point, the hillside dropped away to the level valley floor. The buildings of Phoenix lay to the west. At night, the view of the city lights would be breathtaking. *Not bad for an old sourdough.* Some people would go to great lengths to acquire a prime building spot like this. Maybe someone already had.

Circling to the opposite side of the hilltop, Mitch halted when he spotted a flurry of activity on the flat below. Teams of horses pulling Fresno scrapers dug a broad cavity in the ground. A series of stakes outlined what appeared to be a building site. Stacks of lumber lay piled throughout the area.

Something is going on. But what? Mitch hopped back into his car and retraced his route down the hill, then circled around behind it to the far side. Close at hand, the signs of hurried building were even more evident.

Mitch stepped from the roadster and approached a group of men who appeared to be poring over a set of plans. Before he crossed half the distance, a burly worker blocked his path.

"Afternoon," Mitch said. "What's going on here?"

The brawny man folded arms the size of fence posts across his chest. "Who wants to know?"

"Mitchell Brewer of the *Phoenix Clarion*. It looks like you have quite a project under way here. I'm sure my readers would be interested in knowing more about it."

One of the men stepped away from the group. "What's going on?" he called to the man barring Mitch's way.

The worker eyed Mitch. "Wait here," he ordered. He trotted over to the man in the checkered vest. The two conferred for a moment, casting glances at Mitch from time to time. Finally the man in the vest turned back to the others, and the workman walked back to Mitch.

"You're on private property," he said without preamble. "You need to leave. Now."

Mitch sized the fellow up. At about six feet tall, they stood eye to eye. But even though he kept himself in good condition, Mitch knew he would be no match for this bull of a man. "Nice talking with you." He sketched a wave and headed back to his car.

Pointing the roadster's nose in the direction of town, he eased it down the rutted track, barely able to contain his excitement. He was on to something. He knew it; he could practically taste it. Edgar Wheeler might not be around to give him the last bit of information he sought, but he felt sure the building project he had just left would provide the evidence he needed.

He pulled his gaze from the road long enough to glance at his watch. His lips pressed together in a grim smile. He had just enough time to get to the courthouse if he hurried. If there had been a recent transfer of Wheeler's property, and if the name there matched up with the name on the records of the land adjacent, he would be within a hair's breadth of establishing a connection between the property's new owners and those responsible for Wheeler's death.

He pressed down on the gas pedal, and the little car spurted forward. Mitch gritted his teeth against the bone-rattling jolts as the roadster bounced over the rough road. A little discomfort didn't compare to the necessity of tracking down this information. He owed Wheeler that much.

A flash of light caught his attention. Mitch glanced at the rearview mirror in the upper corner of his windshield and saw a touring car pulling up close behind him. It must be someone from the construction site; he hadn't seen anyone else around.

He pulled over to let the larger car pass. It drew up alongside him, but instead of going by, the other driver kept pace, edging the roadster closer to the side of the road. Mitch tooted his horn and waved at the driver to give him more room.

Instead, the touring car inched nearer. *Is he out of his mind?* Mitch turned his steering wheel farther to the right and stepped on the brake. He would give them all the space they needed.

The right front wheel caught in the sand at the road's edge and spun the car around. Mitch gripped the wheel and held on tight until the roadster came to a shuddering halt. One by one, he pried his fingers off the wheel and stepped outside to survey the damage, seething at the other driver's gall.

Out of the corner of his eye, he saw the touring car pull to a stop a short distance ahead. *Good. I'd like to give the fellow a piece of my mind.* He knelt down to examine the wheel. No cracks; that was a relief. He ought to be able to dig it out of the sand and be back on the road in a matter of minutes.

Hearing the crunch of footsteps behind him, he stood and turned. The face of the workman who had run him off the construction site met his gaze. This time he was accompanied by a flat-nosed man, this one even larger than the first. The two took a stance a short distance away.

The burly man spoke first. "The boss doesn't like people sneaking around."

Mitch glared at him. "I'd hardly call stopping by in broad daylight sneaking. But you made it pretty clear back there that your boss doesn't welcome visitors."

The flat-nosed man stepped forward. "He didn't know whether you were bright enough to figure that out on your own, so he sent us to make sure you got the message." He flexed his arms and cracked his knuckles.

fifteen

Mitch lowered himself into the straight chair in Dabney's office with infinite care. He was still prone to get dizzy if he stood for too long. "I don't know what I stumbled across, but it's obviously something they don't want made public yet."

The older man looked at him and shook his head. "Apparently not, from the looks of you. I'm glad nothing's broken, but you aren't going to win any beauty contests for a while. Not with those shiners you're sporting."

Mitch managed a grin, but he didn't dare laugh. He'd already found out what that did to his bruised ribs.

Dabney leaned forward, a somber expression on his face. "Does this have any connection to your other investigation?"

"You know, boss, I'm honestly not sure. My gut feeling is that the whole thing is all wrapped up in the same package, but I can't give you solid evidence of anything."

"If these are the same people and they're willing to kill an old man. . ." Dabney tapped his pen against his desk blotter. "We may be biting off more than we can chew. Do you think we ought to turn this over to the authorities?"

Mitch shifted cautiously in his chair. "At this point, who do we trust? Someone highly placed has to be involved in order to make all this work. Without any idea who that might be. . ." He spread his hands wide. "Who would we go to?"

Dabney nodded and chewed his lower lip. "Do you want to drop the whole thing?"

"No!" Mitch shot up straight in his chair and bit back a cry of pain. "No," he repeated when he could speak again. "Let them get away with murder besides whatever else they may be planning to do? Not likely. I started this investigation, and I mean to see it through."

"All right. But be careful, will you? And I mean *very* careful. I don't want to lose my star reporter. And take a couple of days off first." Dabney's lips curled up in a grin. "With those bruises, you're liable to scare all your informants away."

⁂

"You really ought to be home in bed, not taking me out to lunch." Catherine squeezed Mitch's arm but loosened her grip in a hurry when she saw him flinch. "I'm sorry. I didn't mean to hurt you."

Mitch waved off her apology. "Other than looking like a punching bag, I'm not doing so badly. I still needed to eat, and it was a lot more pleasant being able to look at you across the table. I'm just glad you were willing to be seen with me, considering the way I look right now."

Catherine warmed to the compliment, but her heart twisted in sympathy. "I still think you ought to talk to the police. Whoever did this to you ought to be horsewhipped."

"Are you volunteering? I'm not sure I'm up to it at the moment."

"I just might." Catherine laid her fingers against his cheek with a feather touch. "Why don't you go home and relax? I'll get Mattie to come with me, and we'll check up on you this evening."

Mitch chuckled. "I'm not quite an invalid, but I'd enjoy the—" He broke off and gripped her arm with a pressure that made her wince. "Who is that?"

"Who? What are you talking about?"

"That man coming out of your office building. The one wearing the checkered vest."

Catherine rubbed her arm. "I don't know his name. I've

seen him there a couple of times, but I've never actually met him. Why?"

Mitch quivered like a hunting dog on a scent. "He was out there at the construction site. I'm pretty sure he's the one who sent those two thugs after me."

"The ones who did this to you? And you think he's somehow connected with. . . No, Mitch. I still can't believe that. I thought you'd gotten over the notion that Mr. Showalter has something to do with whatever ugliness is going on."

"But I've already explained—"

"Even if that man did have something to do with what happened to you, that still doesn't prove Mr. Showalter is involved in any way. Assuming that's the case, I'm sure he doesn't have any idea of the man's true character." Catherine brightened. "You want proof? I'll get it for you. I'll ask Mr. Showalter about him right now and show you how wrong you are."

She felt Mitch's whole body tense. "That might not be wise. Whether Showalter is involved or not, if that man is willing to use violence, I don't want you to do anything that could put you in danger."

Irritation at his overprotectiveness warred with appreciation for his concern. Catherine laughed. "All right. I'll keep myself out of trouble, just for you."

❧

Catherine jotted a last note on her stenographer's pad then started to leave Mr. Showalter's office. She stopped in front of his desk, as though a sudden thought had struck her. "I meant to ask you," she said casually. "Who was that man I saw leaving when I came back from lunch? I think I've seen him here before, but I don't know his name."

Mr. Showalter's brow furrowed. "I'm not sure who you mean."

"He's a little on the heavy side. He was wearing a rather loud vest."

Her boss laughed. "Oh, you mean Joe Crombie. He has some property he insists I ought to buy. The land is pretty worthless, though. I've turned him down a dozen times, but he just won't give up. I sent him away with a flea in his ear today, though. I doubt you'll see him around here anymore."

"Ah. Well, that answers my question." Catherine smiled and carried her pad back to her desk to begin writing the letters Mr. Showalter had dictated.

Wait until Mitch heard. It was just as she thought: That horrid man had no connection to Mr. Showalter at all.

She slipped a clean sheet of paper into her typewriter, and her hands froze as a new thought sprang fully formed into her mind. There was no doubt sinister doings were afoot. Likewise, she had no doubt of Mr. Showalter's innocence in the matter. But what if he were being used as a pawn, as Mitch himself once suggested? Could he be the miscreants' next intended victim?

She rolled the paper into place and began transcribing a letter to an investor in Virginia. At least her boss hadn't made too much of her question. His mood seemed to have improved lately. She tapped on the typewriter keys, grateful for the change. It made things much more pleasant around the office.

❧

"Catherine!" Mr. Showalter's strident bellow echoed throughout her small office. "Where's the Miller file?"

Catherine hurried into the adjoining office, stricken at the thought she might have mislaid a vital piece of information.

"Miller is coming to my house for dinner tonight, and I need to refresh my memory on some of the parcels he's interested in buying."

Catherine plucked a folder from the top of the stack on the corner of his desk and held it out to him.

Mr. Showalter stared at the file in her hand, and a wry grin twisted his lips. "Right in front of me all the time. I'm sorry I snapped at you. Maybe the best thing for me to do is take this home and go over it there. Why don't you call it a day, too? There's no point in both of us running ourselves into the ground."

Catherine smiled her acceptance of this peace offering. "That's a lovely idea. I'll just take a few minutes to put things to rights before I leave."

Straightening her desk took little more than a moment. She glanced through the connecting door Mr. Showalter had left open, and her shoulders sagged. Stacks of files, scattered correspondence, crumpled papers. The place was a mess. She might as well stay a little longer and tidy up after him. She would never be able to do it in the morning with him there underfoot. Besides, his brusque attitude had resurfaced. Maybe having things back where they belonged would put him in a better frame of mind tomorrow.

She returned the files to their places in the cabinet and straightened the stacks of correspondence into neat piles. Encouraged by the room's improved look, she took the time to run a dust rag over the desk and the rest of the furniture.

There. She turned in a slow circle, pleased with the results of her handiwork. *That's a definite improvement.*

She gave one final swipe to the desk and noticed the corner of a paper sticking out beneath the edge of the blotter. *Again? No wonder he can never find anything.* Shaking her head over her boss's tendency to shove papers just anywhere, she pulled the sheet out and gave it a quick glance to see where it should be filed.

Her breath seeped from her lungs when the words on the paper registered in her brain. *Now that Wheeler is out of the way, plans for the resort are progressing nicely. What do we need to do next in regard to the dam sites?* A scrawl of a signature followed.

Catherine made it to a chair before her legs gave out on her. Wheeler. Wasn't that the name of Mitch's informant, the one who had been killed?

Scraps of conversation from one of Mr. Showalter's weekend meetings tickled the back of her memory. What was it? Something about an "old geezer" whose refusal to sell his property was holding up the resort project.

She stared at the paper in her hand. No, it couldn't be. It simply couldn't. Yet the words on the page seemed to imply her boss's involvement, if not actually in Wheeler's death, then certainly as an accessory after the fact.

If that were the case, then the note she held could be the very evidence Mitch was looking for, evidence with the power to send Nathan Showalter and his associates to prison. The paper rattled in her fingers, and she realized her hands were trembling.

What should she do? The note by itself wasn't nearly enough to take to the authorities. And would she do that, even if it were? Wouldn't that make her guilty of the very thing she'd accused Mitch of doing—jumping to conclusions?

That could be exactly what happened. Maybe she had made a mistake and drawn an unfounded conclusion based on a few scribbled lines. It would be utterly unfair to ruin a man's life without more substantial evidence.

But she couldn't ignore it. *God, what do I do with this? It's too big for me to handle on my own.* She waited, not terribly surprised when no answer came. She hadn't been on close terms with the Almighty of late.

She had to talk to someone. Mattie? She rejected the idea as quickly as it came. Mattie's honest face would give her away in a minute. She would never be able to hide any suspicions Catherine might plant in her mind.

There was only one person she could think of. She shoved the incriminating paper in her purse, turned out the lights, and left.

⁂

"If I show this to you, you have to promise me it will stay just between the two of us. There's a good chance it may not mean what you might think it does."

Mitch stepped back from his front door to let Catherine enter his modest parlor, a quizzical smile on his lips. "I take it this is not a Florence Nightingale visit."

Catherine's steps faltered. "I'm sorry. I should have asked how you're feeling. It's just that I need your help." She pulled the paper from her purse and thrust it into his hand.

Mitch scanned the note and sucked in his breath. He looked up at her. "Where did you get this?"

Catherine took a seat on the couch and set her purse down beside her. "I was tidying up Mr. Showalter's office and found it under his blotter. I wasn't snooping, you understand. It was sticking out, and I wanted to put it away where it belonged."

"Showalter?" Mitch lowered himself into an armchair. "Then I was right. From what this says, it sounds like he's not only involved, he may the kingpin of the whole operation."

"But we don't know that for sure. There's no name at the top of the note. We can't even be positive it was meant for him."

"I think you're grasping at straws." Mitch looked at the note again. "Who sent it? I can't make out the name."

"It just says Seth, but it's Seth Kincaid. He works at the county recorder's office. I recognize his signature. I've seen it before on letters he's sent."

Mitch stared at her. "You mean he's in regular correspondence with Showalter?"

Catherine nodded, utterly miserable. "But that doesn't mean—"

"You can't keep sheltering the man, Catherine!" Mitch struggled to his feet and began to pace the room. "If he's involved in this, it's more than just a matter of a shady land deal. He's a party to murder."

She felt her temper rise. "That's just it—*if*. We don't know for sure."

"How much more will it take to satisfy you? This note tells us everything we need to know. It seals the man's guilt, Catherine. It's exactly what I needed to blow this thing wide open."

"No!" Catherine jumped to her feet and faced him. "You can't write about it. Not yet, anyway."

Mitch's eyes widened. "You can't be serious."

"You promised me this would stay between us."

Mitch raked both hands through his hair. "You can't ask me to sit on this story. And no," he added in a biting tone, "it's not just to get my byline on the front page. There's more than a headline involved here. What if holding on to this story costs someone else his life?"

"And what if printing it now destroys the reputation of an innocent man?" Catherine jutted out her chin. "What about a compromise? Give me some time to find out whether I'm right or not before you publish a word of this."

Mitch drew in a slow breath. "How long are we talking about?"

"Two weeks?"

"Catherine, there's no way I can sit on it that long."

"One week, then. Seven days to make sure of the facts."

"Wait a minute." Mitch eyed her with a measure of suspicion. "You said until *you* find out whether you're right. Just what did you mean by that? I thought I told you I didn't want you endangering yourself."

"I don't intend to. I'll just poke around a little, look through the files, that sort of thing. Don't you see? I'm in the perfect position to do this. No one will suspect me of doing anything out of the ordinary. If it turns out Mr. Showalter really is innocent, no one ever has to know we thought otherwise."

"And if he isn't?"

She swallowed hard. "If it turns out he's guilty, I'll do everything I can to help prove it."

Mitch shook his head. "I don't know."

Catherine heard the hesitation in his voice and hastened to drive her point home. "Just one week. If I haven't turned up proof one way or the other by then, you're free to do what you like with the story. . .if there is one."

Mitch wagged his head. "I don't feel good about this."

"Please?" She looked up at him imploringly. "For me?"

He scraped his palm across his cheek and sighed. "All right, you win. One week."

sixteen

The wind was picking up. Mitch turned up his coat collar to keep the chill breeze off his neck. Catherine should be coming out any minute if Showalter hadn't asked her to work late again.

A gust of wind tugged at his hat, nearly pulling it off his head. Mitch reached up to grab it and gasped when a bolt of pain shot through his side. He replaced the hat and fingered his ribs gingerly. The effects of his beating would likely stay with him for some time. Even so, he thought, he could consider himself lucky to get away with only a couple of black eyes and some bruised ribs. He could have wound up like Edgar Wheeler.

Thinking about the man who had turned to him for help made his conscience ache worse than his ribs. The truth about Wheeler's death and the reason for it needed to be told. Here he was in a position to do just that, and instead he had agreed to do nothing.

After a night in prayer seeking the Lord's guidance, he knew he had made a mistake in promising Catherine to hold off. Even so, he had given his word.

The door swung open, and Catherine tripped down the stairs with a glad smile. She waved to Mattie, who smiled and headed off in another direction, more than likely to Woolworth's, her favorite haunt.

Catherine joined him, her eyes sparkling. "I pulled a whole stack of files today and went through every one of them. Guess what? Every last thing in there looks perfectly aboveboard.

I didn't see the slightest hint of anything amiss." She led the way down Jefferson, practically skipping in her exuberance.

"Isn't it wonderful?" she continued. "I'm so glad we decided to wait before we said anything, aren't you?" When he didn't answer, she looked up at him. He could see the sudden shadow of doubt in her eyes. "Aren't you?"

Here it came, the moment he dreaded. "Actually, I'm not."

Her brows knitted together. "But—"

"I made a promise to you I had no right to make. I knew the Lord hates lying lips. I should have realized that applies just as much to covering up the truth."

"Wait a minute. I didn't ask you to cover up anything. We just want to make sure of the truth before you write your story."

Mitch shook his head. "I keep thinking about Edgar Wheeler and what it must have been like when he died. Having just had a taste of being beaten, it isn't something I would ever wish on anyone else." He set his mouth in a grim line. "These people have to be stopped."

Catherine's eyes grew wide. "You mean you're going back on your word? You're breaking your promise to me?"

"No, I won't do that. I already made one mistake. I won't compound it by making another." He paused. "But I do want to take a step back in our relationship. I need to be sure I'm not adding one more mistake to the list."

Catherine stopped short in the middle of the sidewalk. "What do you mean?"

He steered her out of the way of the other pedestrians crowding the sidewalk, hating what he was about to do. "Maybe I was jumping the gun, but I dared to dream of sharing a future with you. But that means being in the same harness and pulling together. Right now, I'm not sure we're headed in the same direction."

Catherine's features twisted in a stricken look that pierced his heart. "So what are you saying? You don't want to see me anymore?"

"That isn't it." He couldn't bring himself to admit to her that he'd considered that very thing. "I don't want to lose our friendship. That has become very precious to me." He drew a deep breath and steeled himself to go on. "But I think we need to let go of any thoughts of our relationship becoming any more than that."

They reached the boardinghouse, and Catherine stared at a point somewhere beyond him. Tears pooled in her eyes, and her lower lip trembled. Mitch longed to reach out and brush the tears away, to kiss those sweet lips, but he commanded himself to keep his hands at his sides.

After a long moment, Catherine blinked and forced a wobbly smile to her lips. Mitch could see the effort it cost her.

She lifted her chin and faced him squarely. "I can't say I understand why you feel this way, but I know I don't want to lose you as a friend. If that's the way it has to be. . ." She gave a laugh that sounded suspiciously like a sob. "I guess we're just friends, then." Her face crumpled, and she walked inside the boardinghouse without looking back.

✦

Catherine leaned over her desk and read the letter from her grandmother for the third time since she'd received it earlier that morning. In it, Grandma expressed her excitement about being on hand for the Admission Day festivities. Then she added: *Are you still planning to come up here and drive us back to Phoenix, or should we make other arrangements?*

Catherine groaned. How could she have forgotten all about mentioning the possibility of a motor trip to Grandma? On the other hand, why should it surprise her? Nothing was going as it ought to at the moment. Coming on the heels of Edgar

Wheeler's death, her discovery of the incriminating note from Seth Kincaid, and now her estrangement from Mitch, the long-awaited announcement of Arizona's admission to the union had faded in importance, something she would never have believed possible only a few short weeks before.

Grandma sounded as excited as ever though, and why shouldn't she? It wasn't her life that had turned upside down. Catherine pictured the delight a long car trip would bring her grandmother and the disappointment she was bound to feel at finding out it wouldn't happen.

She pressed the heels of her hands against her forehead. Just one more example of her ability to let others down. She would have to call the Prescott post office and get someone to relay the message to her grandparents. By the time the story passed from hand to hand, half the people in town would know how she'd hurt her grandmother's feelings.

Wait a minute. Catherine lifted her head and stared at the opposite wall. Mitch had made it abundantly clear he considered their fledgling romance over, but he also said he wanted them to remain friends. Maybe an errand of mercy would fall within the limits of his definition of friendship.

She went to the office phone and gave the operator the number for the *Clarion.* "Mitch Brewer, please," she said when a tinny voice answered.

Her fingernails tapped against the phone cabinet while she waited for him. The voice in her ear made her jump. "Brewer here."

"It's Catherine." She closed her eyes and breathed a quick prayer. "Do you remember offering to borrow your boss's car to bring my grandparents down for the statehood celebration?"

She could picture the play of emotions on his face while she waited for his answer, a slow, drawn-out yes.

Catherine squeezed the earpiece so hard her knuckles ached.

"Is that something you'd still be willing to do. . .for a friend?"

The tone of his voice softened. "I'll check with Mr. Dabney and see what I can do."

⁂

Catherine directed Mitch over the last stretch up the length of Lonesome Valley and drew in a long, deep breath when he pulled Mr. Dabney's touring car to a stop in front of the clapboard ranch house. She sat motionless, drinking in the sight of her childhood home, then felt a broad smile slide across her face. "Welcome to the T Bar."

The ranch house door burst open, and Ben bounded down the front steps. "The prodigal returns! Welcome home, Sis." He wrapped her in a bear hug, then extended his hand to Mitch. "I'm Catherine's brother, Ben."

"Mitch Brewer."

The two men exchanged handshakes and appraising looks before Ben said, "We'd better head into the house. Mom and Dad are champing at the bit." He waited until Mitch turned toward the steps then gave Catherine a thumbs-up. Leaning over, he whispered, "Not bad. This one looks like a keeper."

"I'll be right there," Catherine said. "I need to get my purse." She dropped behind and clapped one hand over her mouth. A keeper? Oh, no. Why hadn't she realized how her family was bound to take her showing up on the doorstep with a young man in tow?

She retrieved her purse from the front seat and trotted up the steps. Then again, maybe it was only Ben. He'd always been quick to jump to conclusions.

Introductions had already been made by the time she joined her family. She had just enough time to see Mitch talking to Ben in front of the fireplace before she was swept into her mother's embrace. "It's so good to have you home, darling," her mother whispered against her hair.

Her father was next. Catherine leaned into his hug and rested her cheek against his chest for a moment, breathing in the scent of the outdoors she always associated with him.

"How's my girl?" he asked.

Catherine gave him a bright smile. "I couldn't be better."

She looked over his shoulder and caught sight of her mother looking at Mitch, then exchanging nods with Ben. Her heart sank. It wasn't only Ben who assumed she and Mitch were an item.

What could she do? She could hardly mortify them both by making an announcement to the effect that there was nothing between them, let alone explain why. All she could do was put up a good front and hope she could carry it through until they left in the morning. She only hoped Mitch didn't pick up on the signals that flew around the room like a flock of swallows.

"Where are Grandma and Grandpa?"

"Alex is bringing them out in the buggy," her father said. "They ought to be here any time now."

Her mother looked at her proudly. "I can't tell you how excited they've been ever since you called. This was a wonderful idea."

Catherine smiled, hoping her impulsive offer wouldn't turn into a major embarrassment for both her and Mitch.

The buggy rattled into the yard moments later. Alex sprang from the seat and helped the older couple down.

Grandma gave Catherine a quick hug then hurried over to the car. "So this is what we'll be driving back in? What a lovely thing for you to do, you and your. . ." She broke off, her gaze fixed on a point beyond Catherine's shoulder. "This must be—"

"This is Mitch Brewer, Grandma. Mitch, my grandmother, Mrs. O'Roarke."

Mitch tipped his hat. "How do you do?"

Grandma's eyes gleamed, and she turned half away from

Mitch to give Catherine a wink. "Let's go inside where it's warmer, shall we? These old bones don't take the cold like they used to." She left them to join the rest of the family on the porch.

Alex remained beside the buggy until the flurry of greetings ended. Then he stepped forward and took Catherine's hands in his. Assuming a mournful expression, he said, "What a shame. I got rid of my ant collection just before I heard you were coming." He tweaked one of her curls and grinned. Catherine made a face at him.

"Then I heard old Mitch was coming with you," Alex went on, "and I knew I had to be here to say hello to both of you." He gripped Mitch's hand. "It's great to see you! Who'd have thought my letter would have wound up bringing you two together like this?"

Catherine sought the refuge of the house before Mitch made his response. "Ben, why don't you help move Grandma and Grandpa's bags over to the car?" She turned to her grandmother. "Are you sure you packed everything you'll need?"

"Everything and then some," her grandfather put in.

The older woman's eyes danced. "I even brought a gown for the statehood ball and made your grandpa pack his best suit. We used to have grand balls at my home in Philadelphia when I was growing up, but I haven't attended an event like that since my youth." She looked straight at Catherine. "You are planning to go, aren't you?"

Catherine stretched her stiff lips into what she hoped was a convincing smile. "Sure, Grandma. I wouldn't miss it."

Her father called out, "You can get those bags later, Ben. Your mother is calling everyone in to supper. We need to get things settled for the night so our travelers can make an early start in the morning."

❧

"I think that's everything." Alex helped Mitch tie the O'Roarkes' luggage onto the back of the touring car and leaned against the fender. "So how are things going between you and my 'little sis'? As if that wasn't pretty obvious," he added with a grin.

"It isn't what you think." Mitch propped his foot up on the running board, glad for the chance to confide in his friend. "I thought we had something special, but. . ."

"Want to talk about it?"

Mitch looked down at the ground then nodded. He poured out the story of their disagreement, leaving out names and specifics of the investigation that brought their relationship to a standstill. His voice trailed off. "I felt like we'd really connected, but I guess I was wrong. We just don't see eye to eye on matters of honor."

Alex let the silence stretch out before he responded. "It's there. I've known Catherine all her life. Maybe this move to the city has knocked her for a loop, but I'm willing to bet it's just temporary." He landed a light punch on Mitch's shoulder. "Give her some time. She'll come around. I'd bank on it."

seventeen

"I'm so glad you came, Grandma." Catherine settled herself in the overstuffed chair in her grandparents' room at the Bellmont. Their obvious pleasure in the brocade wallpaper and elegant furnishings made her glad she hadn't reneged on her promise to them.

"I'm glad, too." Her grandmother tested the mattress of the four-poster bed and gave a nod of approval. She sighed as she sank into the chair opposite Catherine's. "I'm a bit more tired than I'd like to admit, but I wouldn't have missed it for anything."

"I'd better leave, then, and let you get some rest." Catherine started to get up, but her grandmother held up her hand.

"No, stay awhile. I want to talk to you while we have some time to ourselves. Your grandpa won't stay out looking the town over forever."

Catherine resumed her seat, wondering what was coming.

"What's troubling you, child?"

"Me? Why, nothing. I'm having a marvelous time being here with the two of you."

"It's no use trying to hide it from your grandmother. I may be getting up in years, but I still have eyes like an eagle's and the tenacity of a bulldog. Even more, to hear your grandfather tell it." She chuckled then regarded Catherine steadily. "What's wrong?"

"Oh, it's nothing, really. Things have been busy at work, and I have a lot on my mind. I'm sorry I let it intrude on our time together."

"Ah. And here I could have sworn it had something to do with you and Mitch. I thought at first there was something between the two of you. But then I wasn't so sure. Which is it?"

Catherine shrugged. "First there was; now there isn't." She gave a wobbly laugh. "You're right on both counts."

"I see. I wondered what was going on, but I didn't think it was my place to ask, although your grandfather says that never stopped me yet." She tilted her head to one side. "So what happened?"

"We. . .disagreed on the proper way to handle something. Mitch felt our difference of opinion was serious enough that we shouldn't be anything more than friends." She closed her eyes against the sting of tears. Just voicing the fact brought home the finality of their situation.

"And do you think he was wrong?"

The question took Catherine aback. "I'm not sure. What do you mean?"

Her grandmother folded her hands and settled back in her chair. "Let me ask you something else you'll probably think is none of my business. Setting talk of your relationship with Mitch aside for the moment, how are things going in the rest of your life? Church, for instance."

The breath *whooshed* out of Catherine's lungs. She should have expected that. When her grandmother insisted on attending a worship service that morning, she had taken them to Mattie's church, little dreaming the pastor would greet her effusively and comment on her prolonged absence.

"Well," she began, "I haven't had much time. I've been so busy. . . ." She hung her head. "I guess I haven't done too well in that department. But that doesn't mean I'm not close to the Lord." She looked earnestly into her grandmother's eyes. "I don't have to be sitting in a pew to worship Him."

Her grandmother nodded, unperturbed. "That's very true.

However, it strikes me as a symptom of what may be wrong. The Bible tells us not to forsake assembling together, and there's a reason for that." She pressed her palms together then spread them apart. "Just like a coal pulled from the fire will quickly lose its heat, when we let ourselves be pulled away from spending time with other believers, we can lose our fervor for God. Once that happens, it's easy to let attitudes slip into your life that you never would have allowed there before."

Catherine stared, wide-eyed. "And you think I've let that happen to me?"

"I'm not the one to determine that. I'm just saying that when your standing with God is on solid ground, you can trust Him to take care of your other relationships as well." She pursed her lips. "You say Mitch is a man of integrity. Has he done anything to act in a way contrary to that?"

"No. Well, maybe. And that's my fault."

Her grandmother raised one eyebrow.

Catherine let her breath out in a long sigh. "I can't give you all the details. I asked him to wait on breaking a story he felt needed to be written right away."

"And was it important for the story to come out that quickly?"

Catherine squirmed in her chair. "It was more than the story, you see. We disagreed on the way to handle some of the facts relating to it, things that could cause a lot of problems for innocent people if they weren't dealt with correctly."

Her grandmother nodded. "That's a serious issue. Have you resolved it?"

"Not exactly." Catherine heard the tremor in her voice and swallowed hard. "I asked him to give me time to figure out the right thing to do. He agreed, but he felt like he compromised himself by doing that."

"Then you need to make up your mind to follow the right

course of action, and I have a feeling you already know what that is."

"I have a feeling you may be right."

When Catherine stood to leave, her grandmother rested a hand on her arm. "Remember this: No matter what you decide, I will always love you. And I'll be praying for you."

❧

"Are you ready to leave?" Mattie peeked around the doorway to Catherine's office.

"No, you go ahead. I'll be along later."

Mattie stepped inside and leaned against the doorjamb. "Mr. Showalter isn't having a meeting tonight, is he?"

"No." Catherine shook her head. "I just. . .have some things I need to take care of."

Mattie scanned the painfully neat desk. "Uh-huh. I can see you have scads of work to do."

Catherine pressed her lips into a thin line. "It may not look like it to you, but I have plenty of work to see to, and I need time alone to do it."

Mattie planted her fist on her hip. "What's wrong with you? You've been jumpy ever since you went out to run that mysterious errand of yours after lunch."

"I can't tell you right now." She glanced at the connecting door to Mr. Showalter's office and lowered her voice. "Mattie would you just leave now? Please?"

"Okay, okay. I'll lock up when I leave. See you at dinner, assuming you make it home by then." Her quick steps clicked along the hallway floor as she went out.

Catherine leaned her elbows on her desk and pressed her fingers against her eyes. She hated having Mattie angry with her, but there was no help for it. What she had to do would be hard enough without any of her coworkers around.

Help me get through this, Lord. A sense of calm settled over her, the first she had experienced that afternoon. It felt good to be back on speaking terms with the Lord.

Most of the night before had been spent thinking about what her grandmother had said, getting her spiritual house in order, and wrestling with the choices set before her. It took long hours of prayer and a flood of tears, but at last she reached her decision. She barely settled her head on her pillow before the first faint fingers of light crept through her window.

Grandma had been right: She knew the truth. In her heart she guessed she'd known it all along. And with that knowledge came the certainty of what she needed to do.

After the long struggle ended, she thought she would experience a measure of peace, but setting out on her "errand," as Mattie called it, proved to be one of the most difficult things she had ever done. She had managed it, though. The die was cast—she'd seen to that. Now all she had to do was wait.

She heard Mr. Showalter moving about his office, and her breath caught in her throat. He couldn't be getting ready to leave! Not yet.

A knock rattled the front door, and she breathed again. The time had come.

ع

"Go ahead, Miss O'Roarke."

Catherine looked at the tall man beside her, seeking to draw assurance from his air of authority. She glanced past him to the group of uniformed policeman, then nodded and swallowed against the knot building in her throat.

She had tried to prepare herself for this moment all day, but how could a person ever be prepared for playing the role of a traitor?

She tapped on the heavy office door then stepped inside. "There's someone here to see you."

Mr. Showalter looked up and frowned when the men crowded

through the door behind her. "What is all this?"

The tall man reached inside his overcoat and withdrew a folded paper. "I'm Randall Donovan from the district attorney's office. I have a warrant here for your arrest for complicity in the murder of Edgar Wheeler."

Catherine watched her employer closely, wondering what his response would be. She had imagined shock, fear, anger. To her surprise, he seemed utterly unruffled by the news.

He rose calmly and faced his visitors, then glanced down at his desk and picked up a stack of files. "Catherine, would you mind putting these away while I visit with these gentlemen?"

She felt the blood drain from her face. This was not the response of a guilty man. *What have I done?* Sick at heart, she crossed the office and reached out to take the files from him.

Before her fingers touched them, she saw the folders drop to the floor. Mr. Showalter lunged forward and seized her by the wrist. Whirling her around, he twisted her arm behind her and pulled it up tight behind her back.

Pain seared her shoulder when he jerked her toward him, and Catherine cried out. Then she saw a flash of metal and felt the edge of a blade pressed against her throat.

The policemen started forward then froze when they saw the knife.

Showalter's voice lost nothing of its calm. "If you gentlemen would be so good as to move away from the door, this young lady and I would like to leave now."

Catherine heard a whimper gurgle from her throat. Mr. Showalter pulled her arm higher, and she bit her lip until she tasted blood.

Donovan leveled a steady gaze at him. "Let her go and come quietly, Showalter. You're only making it worse for yourself."

"So you say. I think I'll take my chances." His voice sharpened. "Stay back, now. We're leaving. Don't make a move, or you'll have this girl's blood on your hands."

He pushed Catherine forward. She tried to make her numb legs move.

"You're not going anywhere," Donovan barked. He made a sharp gesture. "Take him, men."

Catherine felt the knife blade tighten against her throat and closed her eyes, praying that death would be mercifully quick. Instead of dragging her farther, Showalter shoved her forward into the knot of men, then bolted for the door.

Catherine collided with the grim-faced policemen, and they landed in a tangle of limbs. She heard feet pounding down the hallway, then the sounds of a violent scuffle.

A voice called back, "We've got him, Mr. Donovan."

"Good. Hang on to him." Donovan got to his feet and helped Catherine up. "Are you all right?"

She nodded, cradling her right arm. Her shoulder felt like it was on fire.

"Thanks for your help. We need more citizens like you. We've been looking his way for some time, but we didn't have anything solid to go on until you contacted us. We'll need your help going through the files tomorrow. Will you be up to that?"

Catherine nodded again, unable to find her voice. Mitch had been right all along. If she were honest, she'd had plenty of doubts herself once she saw that note from Seth Kincaid.

She summoned up a tired smile. "I'll be fine. I found some other things this afternoon while I was waiting for you. I'll show them to you then."

She let Donovan out and started to pick up the papers the men had strewn across the reception area in their struggle. Then she dropped them back where they lay. She could take care of it later. All she wanted to do now was go home.

She locked the door behind her and set off on the familiar

route along Jefferson. No Mitch stood waiting for her, but then she hadn't expected him to. Those days were a thing of the past.

Tears burned the backs of her eyes. She had done the right thing—finally. She ought to feel glad of that. But all she could think about was what her delayed actions had cost her.

eighteen

"They dedicated the building eleven years ago. There was supposed to be a copper dome on the top, but the money ran out. Maybe they'll add one someday."

Catherine led her grandparents around to the front of the capitol grounds, where a crowd was gathering in anticipation of the official word that Arizona had become the nation's forty-eighth state.

"That's quite a building." Her grandfather peered at the imposing edifice. "See that stone on the second and third floors? I hear that came from up our way in Yavapai County."

While he wandered off for a closer look, Catherine's grandmother looked at her keenly. "Are you all right, dear? You look a little peaked."

"I'm fine, Grandma."

A tiny furrow formed between the older woman's brows. "Are you sure? You had to work so late last night. I was worried about you being rested enough for today."

"I can handle a short night now and then. I'm fine, really." Her grandparents had heard nothing about Monday's uproar at Southwestern Land and Investments, much less the long hours she'd spent on Tuesday assisting Mr. Donovan in his detailed scrutiny of the company's files. If Catherine had her way, they never would.

So far, she had managed to keep the newspapers away from them. Eager to let the nation know its newest state wouldn't stand for corruption, the papers were full of the story, and Mitch's byline appeared on the most talked-about reports.

It seemed Nathan Showalter and his band of friends had even higher aspirations than profiting on land deals and building resorts. An elaborate scheme had been uncovered to gain control of the water rights to the entire southern part of the state, a venture that, if successful, would have assured them of wealth comparable to the robber barons of old.

According to the talk around town, the speed with which that information came to light was due to the investigative efforts of one Mitchell Brewer, who seemed to know what was going on almost as soon as the story broke. Catherine knew that was due to the research he'd been doing all along, the research she had rejected at first and then tried to get him to squelch.

The knowledge left her numb. The one emotion she was capable of feeling was gratitude that he'd kept her name out of the papers.

Her grandfather called and pointed toward the capitol building. They strolled over to join him. "Look," he said. "Isn't that your young man over there?"

Catherine's gaze followed his pointing arm, and she immediately spotted Mitch standing near the broad front door. He glanced her way, and their gazes locked.

With all her heart, she wished she could make the rest of the world go away, that she could somehow speak a word that would cause this crowd to fade into the distance. She needed to talk to him, to tell him how sorry she was, to admit that he was right.

She could never undo what she had done, and they would never regain their former closeness. But it would be nice to make him understand how badly she felt and know he'd truly forgiven her.

Mitch picked that moment to make his way toward them.

Catherine held her breath and watched him weave through the crowd. Maybe she could find some excuse for them to slip away from her grandparents long enough to tell him what was in her heart.

Her pulse quickened. Grandpa wanted to see the inside of the capitol building. He'd mentioned it just that morning. She could send them along and tell them she'd catch up in a few minutes. It wouldn't take long to say what she wanted to.

Then Mitch stood before them. He greeted her grandparents and turned to her.

"I was hoping—" he said.

Catherine spoke at the same time. "I wanted to—"

They broke off and laughed awkwardly. Mitch nodded. "You go first."

She caught a quick breath and began again. "I thought maybe—"

"Brewer!" A man she recognized as Lucas Dabney pushed his way through the crowd. "Bryan just arrived. If you want a chance at an interview before he speaks, you'd better get moving."

"Right away, boss." Mitch looked back at Catherine, an apology in his eyes.

She waved her hand. "Go ahead. You have important things to do." She watched him hurry off to speak with the great orator William Jennings Bryan while she was left to try to piece her heart back together.

Mitch had a great future ahead of him. He would always be in the middle of things, recording history as it happened. Her heart swelled with pride at the thought of being able to count him as her friend. She only wished he could have been more.

She remembered her grandparents standing quietly at her side. "Let's go see if we can look inside the capitol, shall we?" She led the way toward the massive building. These two dear people deserved to enjoy such a special day despite the pain of her own loss.

⁊⁊

"You look lovely, dear."

Catherine knew she looked more like something the cat dragged in, but she tried to inject a merry tone into her response. "You're the one who looks beautiful tonight." It was true. Lamplight glinted off her grandmother's silvery hair, and her eyes held a gleam of anticipation.

"I'm glad we came," Catherine said and found she meant it. Grandma had done so much for her, and there was so little she could do to repay her. Spending the evening at the statehood ball was a small sacrifice if it helped to achieve that end.

She looked around at the strings of lights hung between the trees, giving the outdoor setting the effect of a twinkling fairyland.

"Isn't that Jim and Nettie Roberts?" Her grandfather gestured toward a couple on the opposite side of the crowd of merrymakers.

Grandma squinted her eyes. "I do believe you're right. Let's go see them." She turned to Catherine. "Do you mind? They're people we knew back in the early days, even before your father was born."

"Go ahead," Catherine told them. "I'll be fine right here."

She watched the dancers swirl, wondering where they found the energy after the rest of the day's celebration. Left to herself, she would have spent the night holed up in her room, alone with her dismal thoughts.

"Good evening, Miss O'Roarke." She turned to find Randall Donovan at her elbow. "I'm glad to see you're able to enjoy the evening's festivities. You've had a busy week."

Catherine managed a smile. "So have you."

Donovan gave a satisfied nod. "We've accomplished a lot.

Once we started picking those fellows up, some of them couldn't keep their mouths shut." He slanted a grin at her. "Your boss sang the loudest. We got the whole story, enough to put the lot of them away for a long time."

"That's good."

"It is indeed. So what are your plans for the future?"

Catherine laughed. "Now that I'm unemployed, you mean?" *Along with the rest of Southwestern's employees, thanks to me.* "I really haven't thought that far ahead."

The future didn't seem to matter much. She had enough trouble dealing with the present.

Donovan lowered his voice. "If you're interested in a job with the district attorney's office, I'd be glad to give you a recommendation. We don't often come across people with your brand of integrity."

Catherine laced her fingers behind her back. "Thank you. I'll think about it."

"Just get in touch. You know where we are." He dipped his head and strolled away.

She shook her head as she watched him make his way through the throng. No matter what Mr. Donovan might think, she hardly considered herself a heroine. She felt deeply grateful to have finally found the courage to act on what she knew was right. And she was glad to be able to help bring the criminals to justice. Still, it was a hollow victory without Mitch at her side.

What did the future hold? She could take Donovan up on his offer, she supposed, and stay in Phoenix. Or maybe it would be better to go back home. Try as she might, she couldn't make up her mind. For one thing, Mitch would be there in the capital. They would be bound to bump into each other now and again. How would she cope when that happened?

Like now. Her heart nearly stopped when she saw him step into the circle of light on the far side of the dance floor. He looked around as if searching for someone.

Should she stand her ground or duck into the shadows? Catherine found the choice was no longer hers to make. Her feet seemed to have taken root, holding her fast.

She couldn't tear her gaze away from Mitch. She watched his every move and knew the moment he caught sight of her. His expression changed, but she couldn't tell what was going on in his mind.

Helplessly, she watched him approach, skirting the dancers, making his way to her. Only a few hours ago, she had longed with all her soul to have a few minutes alone with him. Now she dreaded the coming encounter.

And then he stood facing her, his features solemn. The silence seemed to hang between them for an eternity. Finally, he spoke. "I'd like to talk to you, but there's too much noise here. Would you mind coming away a bit?"

Catherine nodded. *As long as my feet will move.* She found they functioned perfectly well, following Mitch around the corner of the building to a quiet spot. He led her to a bench under an ash tree.

She seated herself at one end and clasped her hands tightly in her lap. At last she found her voice. "You did a wonderful job on those articles."

"Thanks. Most of the groundwork was done ahead of time. But you already know that."

"I appreciate you keeping my name out of it."

"I was glad to do it." Mitch shifted on the bench. "I want you to know how much I admire you for what you did. I know it wasn't easy."

Catherine held back a sob. *Is this all we're going to do from now on—hold polite conversations? This won't work, Lord. I can't just be friends. It hurts too much.*

She drew a ragged breath. "I'm just sorry it took me so long to do it. You were right. I should have listened to you."

Mitch shook his head. "I should have known you would do the right thing. And I never should have pushed you so hard. After all, I got a story out of it, but it cost you your job."

"Well, there's some good news to go along with that. I just had a job offer from the district attorney's office, of all places." She forced out a laugh. "I'm not sure I'm ready to jump into that just yet."

She looked straight at Mitch. "I have even better news. It took a lot for God to get through to me, but I realize I can't put Him on the back burner anymore. If He isn't the main focus of my life, I'm bound to keep making mistakes like that, and I don't want to let that happen. I thought you'd be glad to know I'm back in good standing with Him." Her lips curved. "And I plan to stay that way."

Even in the dim light, she saw a joyful gleam leap into Mitch's eyes. "I'm glad to hear that." He rubbed his palms along his thighs and glanced around. "There was something else I wanted to talk to you about."

He stood and walked a short distance away from the bench, then turned back. "I'm not sure how to say this." A slow smile spread across his face. "Or maybe I am."

Walking over to a rose bush, he plucked a sprig from the end of a branch then strode back to the bench. He sat down next to Catherine and dangled the cluster of leaves over her head.

Catherine pressed herself against the arm of the bench. "Would you mind telling me what you're doing?"

Mitch leaned closer. His breath grazed her cheek. "I know this is Valentine's Day and not Christmas," he said. "But do you think you can pretend this is mistletoe?"

Before she could answer, he pulled her into his arms. The touch of his lips on hers was like a searing flame. The world faded away; only the two of them existed. Finally, Mitch pulled back and stared into her eyes.

Catherine laid her palm against his cheek and struggled for air. "Is that the way you kiss a friend?" she asked when she could breathe again.

Mitch cradled her face between his hands. He ran his thumbs along her cheekbones, sending a shiver of delight through her. His eyes darkened, and his voice dropped to a husky note. "I always prayed that my wife would be my best friend," he murmured. "Would you consider being both?"

This time, Catherine pulled his face down to meet hers.

epilogue

"You may kiss the bride."

Catherine watched Mitch lift her veil, the barest trembling evident in his fingers. He settled the filmy cloth behind her head, and their gazes met. The happiness in his eyes matched the joy that rang in her heart. Then he drew her into his embrace, and she lost herself in their first kiss as man and wife.

"Does the best man get a kiss, too?" Alex's voice filtered into her consciousness.

"A short one," Mitch growled with mock ferocity. "And you'd better not enjoy it too much."

Catherine laughed and pecked Alex on the cheek then turned to Mattie, who pressed the bridal bouquet into her hands.

"Congratulations, Catherine." Mattie's eyes shone like stars. "I'm so happy for you. I always knew you two were meant for each other."

"Even when we didn't." Catherine gave her best friend a long hug, then looked at her through a mist of tears. "Thank you, Mattie. For everything."

"I'm glad you asked me to be your maid of honor. You have a wonderful family, and I've enjoyed meeting all the people here."

Catherine noted the direction of her gaze. "Especially the best man?" She grinned when a blush tinted Mattie's face from her chin to the roots of her hair. She leaned close and whispered, "If it makes you feel any better, I think he likes you, too."

Maybe there would be another wedding in Lonesome Valley before long. The prospect filled her with happiness.

❧

Seated next to Mitch, Catherine let her gaze drift around the gathering. One by one, she studied the faces she loved, all those people who had long been a part of her life and now came to witness the beginning of its newest chapter.

Her parents and Ben, who loved and supported her even when they didn't understand her. Their nearest neighbors, Jacob and Hallie Garrett, deep in conversation with Jacob's parents, who had traveled all the way from Tucson to be with her on this day.

And of course, her beloved grandparents. She watched her grandmother, the way she bent over to speak to her husband with a tenderness that seemed to grow deeper with each passing year. Would she feel the same when she and Mitch had been married that long? Probably so. As long as she could remember, people had told her how much she was like Grandma. That hope warmed her.

She reached over and took Mitch's hand. His smile warmed her even more.

Catherine's father rose and lifted a glass filled with juice from the apples in the Garretts' orchard. "A toast to the bride and groom!"

"Hear, hear!" their guests chorused.

Grandma pushed herself out of her chair and stood with her head held proudly. "And to the passage of last week's initiative that finally gave the women of Arizona the right to vote. Maybe now we can get something done in this state!"

Laughter and applause greeted her sally.

Alex stood next. "I'd like to propose a toast, as well." He moved to a spot before the wide front window. "I've known

Catherine all her life. . .and somehow lived to tell about it."

He waited for the snickers to die down, then continued. "Mitch has been a good friend to me, as well. I feel blessed that God saw fit to use me to bring the two of them together. The sun has risen on a new day for Arizona, and a bright future lies ahead."

He raised his glass and held it high. Afternoon sunlight glittered through the window and touched the glass, tingeing the amber liquid with a copper hue. "May God grant these, my dear friends, a future just as bright. A future filled with love, hope, and the challenges they need to strengthen their faith as they walk together all their days. . .in Arizona."

A Letter To Our Readers

Dear Reader:

In order that we might better contribute to your reading enjoyment, we would appreciate your taking a few minutes to respond to the following questions. We welcome your comments and read each form and letter we receive. When completed, please return to the following:

Fiction Editor
Heartsong Presents
PO Box 719
Uhrichsville, Ohio 44683

1. Did you enjoy reading *Copper Sunrise* by Carol Cox?
   ❑ Very much! I would like to see more books by this author!
   ❑ Moderately. I would have enjoyed it more if

   _____

   _____

   _____

2. Are you a member of **Heartsong Presents**?   ❑ Yes   ❑ No
   If no, where did you purchase this book? _____

   _____

3. How would you rate, on a scale from 1 (poor) to 5 (superior), the cover design? _____

4. On a scale from 1 (poor) to 10 (superior), please rate the following elements.

   ____ Heroine   ____ Plot
   ____ Hero   ____ Inspirational theme
   ____ Setting   ____ Secondary characters

5. These characters were special because? _____

_____

_____

6. How has this book inspired your life? _____

_____

_____

7. What settings would you like to see covered in future
   Heartsong Presents books? _____

_____

_____

8. What are some inspirational themes you would like to see
   treated in future books? _____

_____

_____

9. Would you be interested in reading other **Heartsong
   Presents** titles? ❑ Yes ❑ No

10. Please check your age range:
    ❑ Under 18   ❑ 18-24
    ❑ 25-34   ❑ 35-45
    ❑ 46-55   ❑ Over 55

Name _____

Occupation _____

Address _____

City, State, Zip_____

Schoolhouse Brides

4 stories in 1

Complications abound as love is encountered by four young school-marms in bygone days. In *Schoolhouse Brides*, one-room schoolhouses by the Lehigh Canal, on the prairies of Minnesota, amid the Blue Ridge Mountains, and in frontier Idaho are the settings for heartwarming lessons in life and love.

Historical, paperback, 352 pages, 5³/₁₆" x 8"

Presents

Great Inspirational Romance at a Great Price!

Heartsong Presents books are inspirational romances in contemporary and historical settings, designed to give you an enjoyable, spirit-lifting reading experience. You can choose wonderfully written titles from some of today's best authors like Peggy Darty, Sally Laity, DiAnn Mills, Colleen L. Reece, Debra White Smith, and many others.

When ordering quantities less than twelve, above titles are $2.97 each.
Not all titles may be available at time of order.

HEARTSONG
PRESENTS

If you love Christian romance…

$10.⁹⁹

You'll love Heartsong Presents' inspiring and faith-filled romances by today's very best Christian authors…DiAnn Mills, Wanda E. Brunstetter, and Yvonne Lehman, to mention a few!

When you join Heartsong Presents, you'll enjoy four brand-new, mass market, 176-page books—two contemporary and two historical—that will build you up in your faith when you discover God's role in every relationship you read about!

Imagine…four new romances every four weeks—with men and women like you who long to meet the one God has chosen as the love of their lives…all for the low price of $10.99 postpaid.

To join, simply visit www.heartsong presents.com or complete the coupon below and mail it to the address provided.

Mass Market 176 Pages

✂ -

YES! Sign me up for Heart♥ng!

NEW MEMBERSHIPS WILL BE SHIPPED IMMEDIATELY!
Send no money now. We'll bill you only $10.99 postpaid with your first shipment of four books. Or for faster action, call 1-740-922-7280.

NAME _____

ADDRESS_____

CITY_____ STATE _____ ZIP _____

MAIL TO: HEARTSONG PRESENTS, P.O. Box 721, Uhrichsville, Ohio 44683
or sign up at **WWW.HEARTSONGPRESENTS.COM**